All United Together

All United Together

Tom Wilson

Published in 2013 by Wide Margin,
90 Sandyleaze, Gloucester, GL2 0PX, UK
http://www.wide-margin.co.uk/

ISBN 978-1-908860-05-7

Printed and bound in Great Britain by Lightning Source,
Milton Keynes

Contents

Preface   7

The Gentle Assembly   11

The Problem with dinner time   23

Christian insults   35

Is the school as holy a place as a mosque?   45

Are you what you wear?   57

No go zones   67

The cutest child?   77

Drip feeding   87

CONTENTS

What Christmas means to me   97

Afterword   107

Some possible reading   113

Preface

'We're all united together.' This was how a pupil of St. Aidans described her experience of school to a visitor. The visitor was conducting an audit of the school and asked the school council to tell him about how pupils in the school got on with each other. She articulated what many felt; despite their diverse backgrounds, the school is united as one family. They differ in what they believe about many things, including their religious beliefs. But they are nevertheless united, and they try to work through their differences together.

As a committed Christian, I personally find the parable of the Sheep and the Goats in Matthew 25 to be one of the most challenging passages in Scripture. I am very firmly convinced that, as Ephesians 2:8-9 puts it, we are saved by faith through grace, not of works, that this is a gift of God, lest anyone boast of their own actions. I know and believe that my salvation is a gift of God's grace. And yet the power of Jesus' words remains: whatever you did to the least of these, you did for me (Matthew 25:31-46). They were hungry, thirsty, strangers, naked, in prison, in hospital; you cared for them, and in doing so, you welcomed Jesus in. Are our schools such places of welcome?

This book has created a fictional school, albeit one based in fact, in order to stimulate thought about how exactly Christian schools can welcome all who attend: how do we make our schools places where we are all united together? It is the product of my ethnographic fieldwork and research into Muslim negotiation of the Christianity encountered in St Aidans (although that is not its real name). As well the academic work necessary to produce a PhD, I decided that I would write up my research findings as a novel, in a genre some term 'ethnofiction.' In accordance with the conventions of this genre, no person or incident described here is entirely true to life. All names have been changed and I have anonymised the setting, leaving out some of the normal information that might add colour to a novel. The incidents described are mainly either composites or fragments of incidents I observed during my fieldwork. Occasionally they are entirely fictional, but I would argue realistic to the setting nevertheless. Furthermore, I was not in the school as often as this account suggests, nor was life in the school as fraught or full of incidents as there are in this book. I have deliberately compressed things to make it a more readable account.

As well as giving ethnographic 'thick description' (to borrow a phrase from Clifford Geertz), this book also offers reflection on the motivations of Muslim pupils and theological discussion as to how Christians might respond. Some of this discussion is general to school life; other aspects are particular to the situation of a Muslim majority presence.

I leave the reader to discern which is which. Like any good story, the main purpose of this work is to stimulate thought and self-reflection, and I hope all who read it and are connected in any way with schools will be enriched in their practice by what they find here.

Tom Wilson

May 2013

The Gentle Assembly

'It's about yesterday—it's bound to be. Someone's been skitting her because she came out to help me with the assembly.'

'What do you mean?' Chris asked, looking relieved that it wasn't something more serious.

'Well, you weren't in assembly yesterday, were you?' I said, taking a seat and removing my coat. As I signed in at Reception, Barbara had told me that Chris wanted to see me as soon as I came in, and I'd done as she'd asked. This wasn't normal, and so I was intrigued as to what might be going on.

'No, I was on that course, wasn't I?' Chris reminded me, indicating a pile of paper on his cluttered desk.

'Oh, yeah. How was it?'

'Good, gave me some ideas about getting ready for Ofsted when they come.'

'Well, anyway, yesterday's assembly theme was gentleness.' I explained, getting back to the matter in hand.

'Right.'

I leant forward and began to explain. Taking assemblies in St. Aidans has always been one of the favourite parts of my job. Being a vicar and chair of governors of a Church of England Voluntary Controlled Primary School where over two thirds of the pupils are Muslims is a really interesting challenge. And when most of those Muslim pupils are from Somalia and the Yemen, two of the countries that are more hostile to Christianity than most of the world, it just adds an element of uncertainty, and even excitement.

Church of England schools are not known for being confrontationally Christian, and St. Aidans is no exception to that rule. The assemblies I take are what I would describe as authentically Christian without actively trying to convert anyone. That is to say, they are confident expressions of the Christian faith but at the same time are accessible enough that anyone can get something from them, regardless of their own particular spirituality. This particular assembly was on the theme of gentleness. It was part of a series on the fruit of the Holy Spirit, which I'd introduced as a series on Christian characteristics, and explained each week as being about types of behaviour that we should all aspire to. Being gentle is generally thought to be a good thing, after all, and there are plenty of Muslim spiritual writers who espouse it as a virtue, talking about how Mohammad opposed the unnecessary cutting down of trees in Medina and so forth. Gentleness is a great virtue to encourage amongst children in any case, regardless of one's religious views.

12

My assemblies in St. Aidans always follow a similar format. I introduce the theme, then use either a film clip from a cartoon or an activity to explore the theme, and conclude with a time of reflection, introduced as 'now close your eyes and think about...' and a prayer, introduced by 'now I'm going to pray and if you want to join in with the prayer, say "Amen" at the end.' As I said, the intention is to be distinctively Christian but as inclusive as possible, and it seems to work. A host does not need to hide her own identity, but neither should she deliberately make her guests feel uncomfortable. The Christians in St. Aidans love to welcome people of all faiths and none, but they are not going to hide their faith in order to do so.

But I'm rambling now. Apologies. Back to the matter in hand. The assembly I'd taken the day before on gentleness had used an activity. I set up a domino rally, with very large spaces between the dominoes, spaces so large that in order for it to work as a domino rally, someone would have to gently place a domino into each of the gaps. Once it was set up, I asked Carolyn, one of the teachers, to pick a member of her class, and she picked a Yemeni Muslim girl called Asha. Asha had seemed pleased to be chosen—she had put her hand up to volunteer after all, and had smiled with pleasure when she'd managed to put all the dominoes gently in place. She had also managed to make the domino rally fall with a satisfying clatter and she'd received a round of applause from everyone in the hall.

But then out of the blue Asha's dad had been in to see Chris, the head of St. Aidans, with a strange request, and we were trying to work out why. I suggested that probably what had happened was that Asha was being teased for helping me, and in reaction had complained to her father, leading Chris and I to our present discussion.

'That'll be it,' Chris said, 'You're right, she's been called a Christian or something, because she helped with assembly, and so she's gone to complain to her dad about it, and he's come to me.'

Chris looked much happier once the mystery behind it was clear. He's a fairly relaxed guy, in his mid thirties, with a young family of his own. Being head of St. Aidans is a challenge he really enjoys. He's an activist, so the constant problem solving that comes with being a head teacher is something he finds energising. He's skilled at delving behind the presenting issue, which when it comes to the children in St. Aidans can often be linked to Islam, to try and work out what was really going on. But even though he is good at it, and normally relished the challenge, in this case this skill wasn't all that helpful. Just because we understood the reason behind the request, that didn't make the request itself any easier to deal with.

I needed a reminder: 'So what was it her dad said again?'

'Well, he first of all was talking about how Asha wasn't sure about assemblies and was asking him why she had to go.' Chris said, a slightly exasperated expression on his face.

'Yeah.' This was familiar territory. Periodically many children, Muslim or not, objected to assemblies, especially ones that were overly long and cut into break time.

'And then he was talking about whether there could be a special Muslim assembly on a Friday. It would be voluntary or something, and they'd be mixed gender, boys and girls, talking about Islam and maybe having prayers.'

Now this was news to me, and it wasn't good news. 'Sounds a bit confused to me.' I said, frowning as I thought about it. 'Muslims don't pray in mixed groups any more. The very first Muslims did pray with men and women together, but that stopped centuries ago. Anyway, it'd have to go to Governors, this being an Anglican school. And how would it work, being voluntary?' I was full of questions. A vicar encouraging Muslim prayers? While I am in favour of people expressing their own spirituality and developing a relationship with God, I also think that if a school says it's Christian, then it's complicated for us to promote other faiths, especially when Christian parents choose to send their children to us so that we will give them a Christian foundation for life. We want to welcome those of all faiths and none, but when does hospitable transition into being a doormat?

'Yeah, that's what I thought,' said Chris. 'I mean with your assembly, or mine it's easy. The Chair of Governors is doing the church assembly, we're a church school, everyone goes, and he doesn't force religion on anyone. With mine, it's the head's assembly, and there's never any mention of God or prayers, so that fine. But this just worries me.'

I agreed. It was a concerning idea. St. Aidans is a Church of England school, and yes, we fully signed up to the Anglican mantra of being 'distinctive and inclusive,' of providing a Christian environment in which people of any faith were respected and able to grow up safely. But having Muslim prayers on a Friday in school felt like a step too far. It's one thing to give the Muslim staff time to go to the mosque for Friday prayers, but a wholly different thing to have what was essentially a Muslim prayer time in school. I mean, how would it remain voluntary? Peer pressure is a powerful force, and not easy to resist. And since Muslim parents have different opinions about what age their children should start praying, how they should be taught and so on, it struck me that far from solving a problem, in a school like St Aidans, with so many Muslim pupils from so many different countries, all we were doing was asking for trouble, not reducing it at all. Unfortunately this was my problem, just not exclusively my problem.

'Well, it's nearly the end of term—only two weeks till the Christmas holidays,' I said. 'Let's think about it till then, and hopefully we'll have come up with an idea for a way forward.'

'We'll need to,' Chris said. 'He wants it to go to Full Governors next term, and asked me to put it on the agenda. He'll be there, so it's not like we can just forget about it.'

'Yeah, I know we can't. But we don't have to solve the problem now, so let's just think about it for a bit.' I resolved to put this problem on the back burner for now, letting it simmer away as I pondered possible solutions.

'Okay, fine with me,' Chris agreed.

'Was that the only thing?' I asked, glancing at my watch.

'No, there was something else,' Chris added. 'We've got these different quotes for getting the toilets sorted over the holidays. Since we've got delegated powers, I thought we should just make the decision and get it sorted. And after what you said to me about toilets and the incarnation, I knew you'd want it done as soon as.' Chris smiled at me.

'Sure,' I smiled back. 'Quality toilets are at the heart of being a Christian school governor. Love to get it sorted, provided I can get a cuppa first. Do you want one as well? I'll make them, and then let's have a look at all this paper...'

As I made the tea I smiled to myself as I remembered the governors meeting. Chris had been talking about the need to upgrade the toilets and one or two of the church foundation governors were objecting to the cost. I'd weighed in, suggesting that God becoming flesh in Jesus Christ was a clear sign of divine commitment to all things material, including there being decent toilets. I got slightly carried away, as preachers can do, and the incident was etched in Chris' memory as the 'incarnational toilet' discussion. Some things you never live down...

Tea in hand, I did read through the different quotes for doing up the Key Stage One toilets, but it was hard to keep focused. As I said at the famous governors meeting, I do think that every action in school makes a theological statement. I am convinced that our use of the school budget is an important outworking of our faith. Someone once told me that an organisation's budget is their theology through numbers, and I am sure they're right. Thus the decision to make sure the toilets were less smelly was part of our commitment to value children made in the image of God, whose physical well-being was important to us. And it wasn't just complex theology either: children concentrating on not wetting themselves because they don't want to use a smelly toilet aren't children who are ready to learn. There were pragmatic concerns about basic human decency as well.

But while it was great that these toilets were going to be refreshed, my mind was more on Asha, and wondering why she'd got so upset. It didn't really make sense. Whenever I take assemblies that need a volunteer—and I often ask for volunteers because it's a great way of keeping the kids' attention—I always follow the same routine. The first thing is to say I need a volunteer, and that volunteers sit with their legs crossed, back straight and hand up, so I know they want to volunteer. (That's the crowd control sorted.) Then I explain the task, asking them to keep their hand up if they still want to do it, and then I get a class teacher to pick the person. That way the teacher can reward a child in her class. Not much of a reward admittedly, but for some of those attention-starved kids in St. Aidans, even a minute at the front and a brief burst of applause from the whole school could be a real boost. Asha had kept her hand up for the whole time, and had seemed really quite keen to do the activity.

And anyway, the activity itself wasn't exactly Christian. It was just putting some dominoes in a line and then knocking them down. All the kids had been keen to see—they'd done that half sitting up thing, almost on their feet, which they do whenever I do something exciting at the front. And she'd had her applause, her 'well done,' and gone to sit down before we got to the thinking and praying time, so there was no suggestion she'd participated in that bit at all. Maybe I just worry too much, but it did bother me slightly that she'd got upset.

Taking an act of 'broadly Christian collective worship,' as the jargon puts it, in a school where most of the pupils are Muslims and there are only a handful of practising

Christians, is always a challenge. Personally I remain unconvinced by the name. I always think of worship is a free choice; a whole life lived out of gratitude for the grace of God. Of course corporate gatherings are part of that response, but participation should still be entirely voluntary. So I think in terms of assemblies, of everyone gathering for a moment of reflection together, which each individual can access in a way that enhances their own relationship with God. I sort of agree with the idea that school assemblies are a form of civic religious act done in a consciously Christian fashion, but the key thing is free choice. I've learnt how to take such assemblies mainly through making mistakes, which I guess is the best way of learning anything. Some things come down to attitude: 'assume presence but not participation' is my mantra. I always give the kids (and indeed the teachers) the chance to mentally opt in or out, but at the same time part of me wants them to at least hear what I have to say. After all, they are growing up in a country with a Christian heritage. I'm happy to admit Britain isn't a Christian country any more. But it has a Christian heritage, and in a Church of England foundation school it's important that we take Christian values seriously and explain what they are to the kids, and encourage them to adopt them for themselves, especially where they are completely compatible with what they themselves believe. If the parents didn't want a Christian foundation for their children's education, then why pick St. Aidans? There are good county schools in the area, and even one school that is Muslim foundation, so they could always choose those schools. Why pick an Anglican school and then complain that it's Christian and try to make it more Muslim? It just didn't make sense.

This kind of thing is often buzzing around the back of my head, distracting me from what I should be thinking about, which in this case was deciding which firm had the best plan for making the Key Stage One toilets smell pleasant and stay smelling pleasant. Chris and I agreed on a quote, and as I finished my tea, I had to say, 'You know, it still bugs me, this whole assembly thing.'

'What do you mean?' Chris asked, leaning forward to show his concern.

'Well, Asha volunteered to help, and it was Carolyn who picked her. I really don't get what the problem was.'

Chris nodded. 'It must be what you said, though. It's the only way of making sense of it. Probably someone made a comment on yard and she took it personally. Who knows how the mind of a nine year old works. Maybe she was just feeling a bit vulnerable.'

'True.' Sometimes I do take personally things that aren't personal at all.

'And they all know that they don't have to pray. I did a pupil voice exercise the other week, and asked about assemblies,' Chris said, keen to reassure me.

'Oh right?' I was interested now.

'And several of them said, "Tom says in assemblies 'If you agree say "Amen"' and if we agree with the prayer we say 'Amen' and if we don't agree, then we just sit there and think."'

'Well, that's good.' It's a relief to learn that at least some of what you say in assemblies sinks in, even if it's only the permission to opt out and daydream if you're bored. I remember one girl telling me that she liked assemblies because they were 'a break from lessons!' At least they knew praying was a free choice.

'Yeah, I thought that.' said Chris. 'I think we're doing okay. There have been requests for Friday prayers before. A dad asked two years ago, and it never came to anything. I reckon this will be the same.'

'You're probably right,' I agreed. 'But still, we need to be careful. Don't want to upset anyone unnecessarily. And we can't just ignore it completely and assume it'll go away.'

'No, of course not.' Chris added, 'that's why I want to be careful in thinking about what we do. Prayer is such a difficult area to deal with. But let's leave it for now—it's lunchtime and I want to go out on the yard for a bit.'

The Problem with dinner time

While Chris went out on the yard, I headed for the dining room. I do have an office in the school that I use from time to time, but it's easy to spend too much time shut up in the office reading books and not as much time as I could do with the children themselves. I visit classes whenever I can and try and go to the dining room at least once a fortnight, just to chat to the children and get to know them a bit better, as well as finding out what they think about some of the issues I'm interested in. Dinner time is often a good chance for that sort of an informal chat, although it's also manic, with so many different factors in play all at once.

I sometimes wish that the problems with school food were as simple as *Jamie's School Dinners* suggested they might be, as if it all the problems of childhood obesity and poor nutrition would be solved if schools stopped serving overly processed food and simply made everything fresh in the kitchens on the day. The problem was that when we tried that in St. Aidans most of the children were so used to processed food that the fresh stuff didn't look like real food to them. Fearful of change and suspicious of anything different, they simply refused to eat it, and most of it got thrown away. Furthermore, those children who did want home cooking expected food from the Yemen, Somalia, Kenya, Iraq, Afghanistan, Poland, Mexico, Brazil and Croatia, to name a few of the possibilities, and an English attempt at a curry or chilli was something they'd never experienced before. You know where you are with fish and chips, after all.

And that was only one of the problems. Deciding what you want for your dinner is a complicated business when you're nine. Take Scott as an example: he doesn't really like vegetables or fruit. In fact he'd never eaten fruit before he came to St. Aidans aged five, and still doesn't eat fruit at home. He has learnt to cope with the free fruit given out in school, but even then he only really likes bananas. Fresh vegetables remain largely unexplored territory for him. That rules out any dish that has fruit or veg mixed in with it, such as a curry, stew or bolognese. He's a keen footballer, so whatever he does choose has to be eaten as fast as possible to maximise time on the football pitch. This eliminates anything that involves too much chewing, because that would take away time from the beautiful game. To compound the problem, he's uncertain of anything he's not tried before, or anything that looks suspicious, or anything his mates say tastes or looks odd. But at least he's not concerned about whether or not the food is *halal*.

Ahmed has most of Scott's issues with food, although he is grudgingly accepting of some vegetables, and is happy to eat fruit. However, unlike Scott he also has to make sure food is *halal*, permitted under Islamic law. Ensuring he gets this food in St. Aidans isn't really a problem, although it does rule out at least one meal option every day. Ahmed knows what he is and isn't allowed to eat, and when he lines up for his dinner in school, he just makes sure he gets a white meal tray, not a brown one, which makes the fact that he only eats *halal* food visually clear to all the serving staff.

Ahmed and Scott are good mates and the shared adversity of finding suitable food from the options available is a uniting experience for them. I saw them sitting together as I entered the hall, and went over to ask them how their morning has been. Apparently English was easy today. They're planning a story about living on an island. Sir had shown them some pictures of various different islands and they had to write some descriptions of islands and what they would like their ideal desert island to have on it. I was particularly taken with Scott's idea of his island having ten different kinds of trees, including a chocolate tree, which grew every variety found in a tin of Roses. It's these little details that make the marooned experience so much more bearable...

Ahmed was a bit more uncertain about writing a description of an island, since he's not great at English. But when it comes to maths, he's a real whizz, which I guess it's because maths doesn't require so much language skills. English is in fact his fourth language, after Somali, Arabic and Dutch, and he only started learning it when he was about six, when his family moved from Holland to the UK. So if maths is just a number problem, then it's fine. The difficulties start when it's a word problem: if you don't know what a rollercoaster is, then working out how many goes you can have for five pounds when it is 75p a time becomes another English comprehension exercise rather than a maths problem.

But such difficulties were long forgotten, as more urgent matters were at hand. The challenge for both Ahmed and Scott is simple: who can finish first so they can get more footie time in. Ahmed was just ahead of Scott, mainly because he just bit the centre of his tuna sandwiches, ignored the salad and wolfed down the cake. Scott, distracted by the infiltration of a stray piece of tomato in his cheese butties, took longer, as he had to decontaminate before proceeding. But they both still managed to be in and out in less than ten minutes, which is average feeding time at the school dinner trough for boys of their age.

The rush was already clearing by the time the two lads were finished, so I went to say hi to Jane, who would now have the time to talk. Jane is a great school cook, always friendly and smiling, and always doing her best to make sure that the kids get something they want to eat, provided it comes within the confines of the instructions from the catering firm she works for. Portion control took on a whole new meaning when I saw the thin layers of sandwich fillings they were instructed to make. The great thing about Jane is that she doesn't always pay attention to such diktats, preferring the kids to be happy and fed, with a smaller profit margin for her employer, than the profit to be fat and the kid's tummies to be rumbling.

Jane doesn't ever really get worked up by the whole *halal* food issue. She does sometimes talk about 'their food' and 'ours' but such boundary marking is quite common in

St. Aidans. The kids do it all the time, often confusing the difference between *halal* food and Arabic food, or between *haram* (forbidden) and Christian food. Until I came to St. Aidans, I never knew that a bacon butty was in fact a Christian meal!

Jane also dealt very well with the graffiti incident a few years ago. Some friendly person wrote 'F*** off Pakkis' on the gates by the kitchens, and she didn't gossip about it, or make an issue of it at all, simply observing how dense this person was, since there are no children from Pakistan in St. Aidans at all. Although she handled this particular incident with sensitivity and common sense, Jane has always been clear that she doesn't want her kitchens to become completely *halal*. I'm sure she's right that if they were, we'd simply get more of that sort of graffiti and probably much worse. After all, there was a BNP candidate in this area at the last general election. But a good host always makes sure that her guests have everything they need, and that is exactly what Jane does, making sure that all the children she looks after each day get a warm welcome and food they can enjoy.

Sadly not every staff member in St. Aidans is always as understanding. Back when the *Daily Mail* ran some scare articles about *halal* food, a few staff did mutter one or two things to me about how they weren't sure about 'that *halal* food,' declaring that they 'certainly wouldn't eat it, as it would make me ill.' When I suggested that the designation '*halal*' was simply about how the animal was killed, and didn't affect the taste or the quality, they were a bit surprised, especially when I added that sometimes *halal* food is in fact far better quality than some of the factory farmed rubbish some school kitchens get given. This argument about food quality has been deployed effectively at governors' meetings by Muslim parent governors on several occasions, and seemed to work just as well with the staff when I deployed it in response to their concerns.

Food is, I guess, such an emotive issue because it's so personal. We are what we eat, as the saying goes, and possibly eating food associated with a religion you're uncertain about means you come a bit too close to that religion for your own comfort and peace of mind. This confusion has a long pedigree. The seventeenth-century fear that drinking coffee (or 'Mohametan gruel' as they called it) made you into a Muslim may seem absurd now, but the uproar over *halal* burgers in Twickenham is from the same stable, in my opinion at least. A very long time ago the apostle Paul wrote to churches in both Rome and Corinth reminding them that Christians do not need to worry about the food they eat, and before that Jesus himself declared all food clean to eat. Sadly Christians are not always as confident, and British culture has certainly got itself into a bit of a mess about *halal* food at times.

Having thanked Jane for the great job she was doing feeding the children, I went out on the yard for the last few minutes of dinner time, and asked Aliyah and a few of her friends what they'd thought of their dinner. 'It was nice, sir,' was the standard reply. 'Today was tuna sandwiches and I like those.'

'Do you ever worry about whether the food is *halal*?' I asked. I think it's always worth checking this from time to time, and it helps to clear up any confusion before things get too problematic.

'Nah, sir, now we've got the trays it's easy to tell.' It had taken a few false starts to come up with the system of trays. Trying to get children lined up in two groups, *halal* and non-*halal* food never quite worked, and treated the children more as a problem than as people. The trays gave them the ability to express their own choices, and seemed to work much better. It was especially important for a new arrival who spoke little or no English, as it gave them a degree of control over their diet.

'But me brother did once eat a bacon butty by mistake,' one of the girls said.

There's always one person who loves telling shocking stories in any class in the school, and in this case it was Aliyah.

'What happened?' Like an obedient trout, I duly swallowed the tasty bait and bit firmly on the fishing line of her story.

'Well, sir, he was at a friend's house, and didn't realise that it was *haram*, sir.' Aliyah explained. Her grandparents are from the Yemen, although both her parents and all her siblings were born in the UK. She's always worn a headscarf to school, at least for as long as I've known her, and seems to take her faith quite seriously. Food is a significant boundary marker even for quite nominal Muslims, and for someone as devout as Aliyah, avoiding all *haram* (forbidden) food was crucial for her personal piety.

'Yeah?' I asked, interested to see how this incident had been dealt with.

'And his mate gave him this butty with meat in,' Aliyah continued, 'And he thought it was chicken and when he bit it, it was bacon. And because he was at a mate's house, he couldn't not swallow it, so he had to eat it.'

'What the whole sandwich? Did he get into trouble?'

'Nah, it was a mistake, wannit. It was fine. And he only ate one bite, and then asked for another butty. He probably cried—he's always doing that.'

'Oh right. Well, it's good that he didn't get into trouble.' Islam is quite forgiving, especially to the young. Aliyah's brother is currently only seven, so he was probably five or six at the time. I wondered if this was an isolated incident, and so asked the obvious question. 'Has that happened to anyone else?'

'Well actually, sir,' Aliyah's friend Salma said, 'I think a few of us might have been.'

She looked a bit embarrassed, so I realised I had to be gentle. 'Why, what happened?' I asked as kindly as I could.

'Well sir, you know those drumstick lollies?'

'The kind of chewy rectangular ones?'

'Yeah, those. I used to always eat them, but Miss Williams said that they've got gelatine in them and so we shouldn't eat them.'

'Oh really? That's a shame, as they're nice.' I smiled in response to Salma's sheepish grin.

'I know sir,' she continued. 'I didn't think they was a problem, so I used to eat them, but Miss Williams read the ingredients list on them to check, and she said that they do, so we can't have them. I was gutted.'

'Yeah, I can imagine. It must be annoying to keep having to check everything.' I suggested.

'Yeah, it is, sir. But we don't always bother. Because if you didn't know or if it's a mistake, then that doesn't count.'

'Yeah, and if you say "*Bismillah* I hope this is okay," then Allah will forgive you,' added Thanya. 'Allah is merciful, and if you ask in his name, then it is okay to eat sweets you're not sure about.'

That was news to me. Saying 'In the name of God I hope this is okay,' was certainly a novel strategy for avoiding divine displeasure, a sort of preemptive request for forgiveness, if you like. Children are often quite creative in their faith, and I would have loved to explore this idea further but at this point the whistle went for the end of dinner time, so with a quick 'Bye, sir' the girls all ran off to line up to go back into class.

It is all really interesting, I thought to myself, resolving to go and make a cup of tea before getting on with some more work. *Halal* food clearly does work as a boundary marker, but not always in the way you might expect. The kids do sometimes work on the principle that ignorance is bliss, and that if they don't ask whether some sweets might be *haram*, then they probably aren't and so are okay to eat—a policy worth adopting if tasty treats are available. This is in keeping with mainstream Islamic doctrine, which includes a presumption of what I call 'original innocence,' that children are not held accountable for their actions until they reach puberty—quite different from Christian notions of original sin. This is supported by the understanding that if the Quran does not explicitly prohibit something, then it is probably permissible.

Having said that, for some of the kids, *halal* food is a really big issue. There was a bit of an unfortunate incident last Christmas. The year six teacher, Mrs Morgan, hadn't really thought it through properly, and made a pass-the-parcel, with sweets in every layer, something she thought would a great treat for the class party on the last day of term. But she hadn't bought *halal* sweets, and so once the first layer was unwrapped and a Muslim child held up his prize, the other children in his class all said 'You can't eat that, it's *haram*.' And what does any ten year old do in response to that kind of public pressure? He puts the sweets to one side and passes the parcel on. But if no one eats the prizes, then pass-the-parcel becomes a really dull, indeed slightly pointless, game.

The *halal* police can be quite a suspicious bunch as well. Mr Owens, the year four teacher, got himself into trouble with them at the start of the year. Being the conscientious type, he'd made sure the jelly sweets he'd bought as treats were *halal*. Since you can buy them in any of the local cornershops, this wasn't especially difficult to do. Even though he can't read Arabic, they normally say *halal* in English as well, and the Arabic of the *halal* logo on most of them is quite distinctive.

But persuading the more sceptical members of the *halal* police that yes, even though he was a white middle aged Christian man, the sweets clearly labelled *halal* were in fact *halal* was a challenge he eventually grew tired of. There's only so many times you can point out to a distrustful eight year old that it does in fact say *halal* on the packet in Arabic.

It's easier to simply say, 'well, if you want it that way, no treats for you.'

Kamal and Amjad, the *halal* police mentioned above, are two quite suspicious eight year olds, who successfully managed to prevent the whole of their class getting sweets as treats. Both are from Somalia, and both take their faith really very seriously. I've met many Muslims who do (as well as a lot who don't), but these lads are particularly conscientious. They are already fasting regularly, which is slightly unusual for someone of their age, as fasting is generally not assumed to be mandatory until at least secondary school age. But it doesn't really affect their school work, and they're often irritable and grouchy even when they're eating regularly, so fasting only makes that slightly worse. They certainly keep us on our toes, making sure we make it easy for them to fast and provide them with food they can eat, which is a good thing, although their lack of gratitude can, at times, be mildly annoying... And food is only one of the many areas of possible controversy for Muslim boys who are deeply distrustful of their Christian school.

Christian insults

Wednesday started quiet and calm, which was just what I needed to get ahead with preparations for the Christmas rush. One of the great things about my office in the school is that I have a haven of peace and calm with no phone connection or parishioners who want my attention, perfect for thinking about what aspect of the Christmas story I want to focus on during our services this year. So there I was, sitting in my office, laptop open, enjoying the solitude and thinking about fear, how Mary, Joseph and the shepherds are all told to not be afraid, and how one part of the Christmas message is that we don't need to be afraid any more because God is with us, bringing peace on earth.

Glancing out of the window in the response to the shrieks and laughter of break time, all thoughts of peace were pushed from my mind. Kamal and Amjad in year four were engaged in some kind of a minor scuffle. They were hacking away at each other's shins, kicking quite viciously. I stood and turned to the door, but by the time I was outside, Helen Lewis, their Learning Support Assistant, was already there. She marched them off towards Chris' office, and off they went, faces flushed with anger, eyes to the ground, sulks already building.

Being the nosey type, as many vicars are, this was the perfect moment to go and make a cup of tea, and find out what that was all about. The kettle had just boiled when Helen came in.

'Tea?' I offered.

'Yeah, ta. Milk and one sugar please.'

'What was that all about? You know, with Amjad and Kamal?'

'Ah, this time Tom, it was a weird one. Normally it doesn't bother me when they argue and fight, but this time, I got quite cross with them.'

'Really? Why?' Helen is a patient woman. So for her to be cross was quite unusual.

For a good reason, as it turned out. Apparently, yesterday evening, Kamal went to the Lifestyles gym, and saw Amjad's older sister Aisha there. Quite unusually she wasn't wearing her headscarf. Aisha's fourteen, and so now is of an age where, according to her strict Somali Islamic beliefs, to show her hair in public would be *haram*. But she is also a British born teenager, strong willed and sure of her own mind, so such Islamic beliefs don't necessarily mean anything. Maybe, like some Somali girls, she decided not to wear it to the gym, because of how hot she'd get playing badminton or whatever it was she went to there to do. Or maybe she forgot it, or had taken it off for a moment while changing.

Kamal, of course, is eight, and doesn't think very deeply about these things. As far as he was concerned he saw a Muslim girl he knew doing something *haram*, and so decided that meant she'd become a Christian, a fact that he felt it was best to share with as many people as possible. Before I came to St. Aidan's, I'd never heard 'Christian' used as an insult. When it's been accompanied by some kind of a pejorative epithet, or a swearword, then such references do come my way from time to time, as do names like 'Bible basher.' But I've never hear of anyone simply being called 'Christian' to mean 'outsider, scum, beyond the pale.' It's a whole new use of the word that I personally have only encountered from a tiny minority of the pupils in St. Aidans. We all mark boundaries in different ways, and what is a label of belonging for some signals exclusion for others. For Kamal, 'Christian' means 'outsider.' Mind you, it may not be especially significant that he used 'Christian' as an insult, in any case. Kamal had been in trouble earlier in the term for calling two of the other boys 'Taliban,' just because they were recently arrived Afghani refugees (fleeing the Taliban, ironically). Sometimes children just pick up useful labels as easy insults without thinking through the implications of that choice at all. Part of the challenge of a school like St. Aidans is helping them develop the sophistication to think before they speak.

Anyway, Kamal had busied himself at break time telling everyone that Amjad's sister had become a Christian, and Amjad, once he got wind of this, spent the time boiling up the pressure cooker of his anger until it was ready to explode on Kamal. He's quite good at timing it right, managing to build up a great head of steam with just two minutes of break time left. This meant he got a few good kicks in, and also got to miss maths.

'And the thing is,' Helen continued, 'I bet he's in Chris' office right now explaining how in the Quran it's *haram* to insult people or lie about them. I've learnt about this. When I first had this class I used to take it very seriously when they started talking about the Quran. But I've been with them for two years now, so I've learnt. They talk about stuff being *haram* all the time, but often they go and do exactly the same thing themselves.'

'Like what?' I wondered. Hypocrisy isn't unknown in Christian circles either: we talk about loving our enemies, but often find it hard to do that. Was this the kind of thing Helen was talking about?

'Well, lying is a good example. There's many a time I've caught one of them in a lie, and they'll swear blind to me that it says in the Quran it's *haram* to lie, so there's no way they'd ever do that. But they're doing it. So I say to them "You're lying though" and we kind of get stuck there.'

A sticky situation indeed. What do you do if someone says they know they shouldn't lie, but they are lying, other than tell them to stop it? Having to deal with that day in, day out would wear me down, and I wondered if the same was true for Helen. 'Sounds like they're hard work, that lot,' I suggested to her.

'Oh, they're good kids. They can be a bit of a pain at times, and they don't always get on with each other. To be honest I think a lot of them don't really like each other, and this comes out in all sorts of ways. But on their own, they're all great kids, and they can be a great class when they're not too grumpy. I love them really. But this time, I think something does need to be said to them. They can't carry on like this. I hope that Chris can sort them out. Anyway, must get back to class.'

And Helen headed out of the staff room, tea in hand. I sat for a minute, finishing mine, and thought again about the vast difference between doctrinal and lived religion. The teachings of our faith are quite clear, but we often fail to live them out, meaning outsiders develop a really skewed understanding of what we believe. Take loving your neighbour as yourself: no Christian would deny Jesus taught that, but so many Christians spend so much time plotting how to gain advantage over others, how to get what they want at the expense of others, and generally hating their neighbours, that you'd be forgiven for thinking Jesus never said anything of the sort.

Once I'd finished my tea, I headed back to my office to try and think about peace on earth again, resolving to find Chris at lunchtime and see if there was anything I could do to help these children live out the ideals of a more harmonious school family than I'd seen at break today.

As it turned out, there was. And I didn't need to go to find Chris, because he came looking for me. I'd got a bit further with peace on earth, but only a bit, before there was a knock on the door, and Chris came in.

'Hi Tom, you alright?'

I saved what I was typing and looked up. Chris had slipped into my office and was standing by my desk. He was smiling, but there were slight bags under his eyes. 'Yeah, good thanks. You?'

'Bit tired. James was up at four this morning, so I was up early.'

The trials of having a one-year-old baby. 'Ouch. You must be shattered. Don't work too late tonight then.'

'I won't. Did you see Kamal and Amjad today?'

'Well I saw them out of the window. And I spoke to Helen, who said it was something about Amjad's sister not wearing her headscarf and this making her a Christian or something?'

'Yeah, that's it. I spoke to them just now. I've decided to call their parents in and speak with them as well. They keep getting into trouble and fighting, those two. It's got to stop. So I want to speak to mum and dad and get a clear link between school and home. But I wanted to talk to you as well.'

'Why?' It's not normal for me to be involved in this sort of a discussion. Day-to-day disciplinary matters aren't really in the chair of governor's purview, and rightly so.

'When I spoke with Amjad and Kamal, I asked Kamal about why he'd said what he'd said.'

'Yeah?'

'And I said to him "So is being a Christian a bad thing then? I'm a Christian, does that make me a bad person?" And do you know what, he so wanted to say, "Yes". I saw it in his eyes. But he knew that I'm his head teacher, and if he said that he'd be in so much trouble.' Chris shook his head, saddened by what it meant. 'And do you remember what he said to Phil a few weeks ago?'

'I think so. Was that the comment about this being "only a Christian school"?' I asked.

'Yeah, that's the one,' Chris confirmed. That had been a bolt from the blue. Phil had been explaining to Kamal that he needed to think more carefully about his behaviour, that he needed to treat everyone in school with greater respect. Kamal hadn't agreed with him, and had blurted out something like 'Why? It's only a Christian school.' Thinking back, I remembered Phil telling me all about it. 'I was quite pleased with myself,' he'd said, 'I remained calm, didn't shout at him at all. Just sent him out of the class to think about what he'd said.' But from Phil's account, the worrying thing had been the reaction of some of the other pupils. When Kamal had blurted this out, there had been a collective intake of breath from ninety per cent of the class. The vast majority, including most of the Muslims present, were genuinely shocked that Kamal thought like that. But one or two of the boys had just sat there and smirked, Phil had said, as if they agreed and were pleased that someone had finally said what they were thinking all along. At the time we'd had a long discussion about what this had signified, whether this was really what they thought, and why it had suddenly come to light. Phil had suggested it might simply have been the first insult Kamal had been able to come up with, and might not signify deep-seated religious bigotry at all. I could see the sense in his argument, but also recognised that when we speak without thinking we normally reveal some of our inner thoughts, and was a bit concerned that Kamal might have such views about Christians, but I'd never had the chance to take it any further with him. But now the opportunity had arisen.

'Saying it's "Only a Christian school," and suggesting that being a Christian is the worst possible choice you can make. They're definitely sentiments the boys need to keep to themselves if they're going to come here, aren't they?' I said, agreeing with Chris. But I still wasn't quite sure what it had to do with me. 'So what do we do?' I asked.

'Well, I wondered if you could speak with the whole class maybe, and talk about how there should be respect between the different religions.' Chris proposed.

This seemed like a sensible idea. Many Muslims suggest that Islam is a religion of peace, but that clearly wasn't a concept that Kamal and Amjad had got hold of. I agreed: 'Yeah, I can do that, but probably not until next week. Is that alright?'

'Yeah, it'll be fine. And you could come in tonight as well if you want to.'

'Thanks, I will. It makes the whole request for Friday prayers in school a whole lot more complicated as well, doesn't it?' I could sense that this knotty problem was only going to get worse before it got better.

'Oh, I'd forgotten about that.' Chris didn't look as if remembering about it was a good thing. 'It does. Now I've even less of an idea of what to do about it.'

'Well, we said we'd leave it for a week or so, so there's no need to decide anything yet.' I did my best to reassure him, although I'm not sure if it helped much. A problem deferred is still a problem, after all.

'Yeah, you're right. Oh, and the other thing was Fiona in year six has asked if she can go slightly early. It's her son's school play at 2 today, so I said she could go at lunch time. Just so you know. See you later.' He left my office and strode off.

Chris is always good at ensuring staff are well cared for, and also diligent in keeping me updated about the decisions he's made. We have a great working relationship, and I always feel on top of what's going on in the school. I checked my watch, and realised I had just enough time to turn my computer off and head out for the visit I'd arranged. Joe's in his mid fifties, and is still mourning the loss of his wife Marie to cancer. She fought hard against it, but finally lost the battle. That kind of visit really helps me get a perspective on the boys and their arguments, and all the other rough and tumble of school life. It's true that young children can often be accidentally and casually cruel to each other, but often the blows they deal out are still far more gentle than the wounds adults have to endure.

Today Joe was in quite good spirits, and we talked for a while about Marie, and how he missed her and the holidays they'd enjoyed together. Mainly we talked to fill the emptiness of his house, to honour the past, and to help him gain the energy to start a new phase of life—one he'd hoped to never have to live. I left after an hour and a half, feeling tired but pleased to see the progress Joe was making. I headed back to St. Aidans, turning over in the back of my mind what I might want to say to Kamal and Amjad's parents. The biggest worry would be: what if they agreed with Kamal, and thought that being a Christian was the worst possible decision anyone could make? Then we'd really be heading for interesting times.

Is the school as holy a place as a mosque?

I got back to school in time to speak with Barbara, the school admin officer, about Chris' recent pay rise. We'd just done his performance management a week before, and we'd agreed a pay rise that I was quite keen to get through the LEA's system before the end of term, so it would be in his December pay packet. Barbara is a real blessing, highly efficient and organised, so she'd got things all sorted. All I needed to do was sign the relevant form and letters and thank her for a job well done.

While we were chatting about our respective plans for Christmas, a man came to the school gate, and Barbara buzzed him in to the entrance hall. He was quite tall, and had the dark features and prominent brow of a Somali. His beard was well trimmed and neat, his teeth slightly yellowing, and his eyes deep and dark. As he signed in, he spotted my clerical collar and asked me 'Are you the man who takes the religious meetings?'

This wasn't a question I'd been expecting, but I decided that I probably was the man he was looking for, and so answered in the affirmative and then explained, 'Well, I take the church assemblies once a week on a Monday morning. My name's Tom. *Salaam Aleikum*. Pleased to meet you.'

That was about the extent of my Arabic, but it's a vital phrase, a blessing of peace that communicates a clear desire to engage with people on their own terms and in their heart language.

'*Wa aleikum salaam*' he replied, looking pleased to be greeted in this way. 'I am Mr Hussain. I am coming to see Mr Norton. I think I am early. Do you have time to talk?'

I certainly did have a few minutes, and since I was also going to see to Chris Norton, probably about the same thing, it seemed like a good idea to chat. I wondered whether he was Amjad's or Kamal's father, and enquired.

'I'm Kamal's father. He is a good boy.'

'Indeed he is. Sometimes high spirited, but a good boy, as you say. What was it you wanted to ask me about? Let me come round and speak with you.'

I decided the subject of Kamal's behaviour was not one to discuss at the moment, so I steered the conversation to potentially more risky, but at the same time much safer topic. Religion in general, and my religious practice in particular is normally a better topic of discussion that the behaviour of other people's children. I walked round from the school office to the entrance hall, where he was sitting waiting to be let into the school itself. Once I was seated next to him on the dark blue reception chairs, which fill such rooms throughout Britain, he explained his request.

'Ah yes, I wanted to ask about the religious meetings, and what you say to the children, because sometimes they ask me about it, and I don't want them to be confused. There are many things in common between Islam and Christianity, and it is good to talk about these things.'

I concurred that there were many points of common contact, and explained that I didn't take any religious meetings. I added that in my opinion, school assemblies have long since ceased to be acts of worship, even if the official government name for them is 'collective worship.' Collective they may be, but worship they aren't, unless an individual choses to make it worship, which to be honest most of them don't. I think of the assemblies I take as a chance for children to grow spiritually, to experience a dimension that is often missing from their lives, and hopefully to have a bit of fun.

I talked Mr Hussain through a typical assembly, using the one on gentleness I had taken earlier that week as an example, stressing that prayer was always optional, and that the assemblies normally focused on values and character traits that were common to both Islam and Christianity.

'That's very good,' Mr Hussain approved. 'Islam is a religion of peace, and it is good to live in peace with our neighbours? There is a great *hadith* about the Prophet, peace be upon him.'

'Really? What does it say?' The *hadith*, the traditions of the sayings and actions Prophet Mohammed are often informative. They were recorded by different people who were close to him, and handed down, first by word of mouth, and later in edited collections.

'Yes, it is said in the *hadith* of *Bukhari* that a man came to the Prophet, peace be upon him, and said, "I had sexual intercourse with my wife on Ramadan while fasting." The Prophet asked him, "Can you afford to pay for a slave to be freed?" He said that he could not. The Prophet asked him, "Can you fast for two successive months?" He said that he could not. He asked him, "Can you afford to feed sixty poor persons?" He said that he could not. Then a basket full of dates was brought to the Prophet and he said to that man, "Feed the poor with this by way of atonement." The man said, "Should I feed poorer people than we? There is no poorer house than ours between Medina's mountains." The Prophet said, "Then feed your family with it." As the Prophet, peace be upon him, was gentle with this man, so we should be gentle with each other. Gentleness is a good value to explain to children, as they can sometimes be rough with each other, no?'

'They certainly can.' I was relieved to discover that this Muslim parent, at least, didn't think the assembly on gentleness last Monday was a problem.

At that moment the gate buzzed, and two more Somalis came in, a man and a woman this time. She was wearing an *abiya*, a long flowing black garment that covered her from her head down to her ankles. She was also wearing a long skirt, so only her face and hands were visible. Her husband (at least that's whom I assumed he was) was wearing what looked like two coats and a big woolly hat. I guess having grown up somewhere so much warmer, he found the UK winter something of a challenge. Like Mr Hussain he had a neatly trimmed beard and deep brown eyes. As they signed in, Mr Hussain began to talk to them in Somali, and I quickly concluded they must be Amjad's parents. I zoned out, letting the familiar but incomprehensible sounds wash over me as we waited for Chris to come and get us.

It was only a few minutes. Chris came to find us, buttoning up his suit jacket as he came. 'Great to see you all. Do come into my office. Would any of you like a drink?'

The lady declined, but both men asked for tea, with four sugars each.

'You do like your tea sweet, don't you?' Chris smiled, as he ushered us all into his office, and gestured towards the seats. 'Sorry about the mess.'

'Yes, for us tea must be sweet,' Amjad's dad explained. 'And if your office was too tidy, I would worry that you did no work,' he added.

Chris smiled his thanks, assuring the parents that he did plenty of work. While we waited for the tea to arrive, Chris introduced me again and explained why he'd asked the parents to come in, to make sure there was a clear link between school and home when it came to establishing discipline.

The parents all nodded, and looked serious. There was a knock on the door, and Barbara came in with two teas, which the men accepted gratefully. Although both said thank you, neither made eye contact with her; to do so would have been deeply inappropriate as far as they were concerned. 'Thanks, Barbara,' said Chris.

'Pleasure. I'll put the sign up,' she said as she left, closing the door behind her and sticking the laminated "Meeting in progress" sign on the door to give us the privacy such a meeting required.

Chris then continued with his explanation, adding that although there had been an incident involving Kamal and Amjad in school today, that wasn't the main reason for calling their parents in. It was more a cumulative thing: 'there have been so many incidents recently involving the boys, I thought it would be good to just say to both of them in front of you all that they sometimes behave in a manner that's just not appropriate for school.'

'But what happened today?' Amjad's dad wanted to know.

'Well, it's not nice, so I don't really want to say.' Chris hesitated.

'No, we must know.'

And so he explained. As he talked I watched their faces, and the shock on all three was clear when Chris explained the pejorative use of 'Christian.' I'm sure that the horror and upset they expressed was genuine, confirmed by the shift in posture, the widening eyes and the wringing of hands that followed. 'Those boys are in trouble tonight,' I thought, 'and what's more, it's clear that they didn't get any of their anti-Christian sentiments from home. That makes it a bit more confusing. They're not getting it from school or from home. Maybe the mosque? But they go to the one on Williams Street, and I've always thought that's a moderate one.'

I tuned back in to the conversation to hear Chris say, 'Now let's call the boys over and see what they've got to say for themselves.'

Kamal and Amjad were summoned, and while we waited, Chris said, 'Now, I don't just want to call them over to shout at them, as that won't do any good at all. It's so they know that what happens in school does affect home as well, because I worry that maybe they forget that, and think they can do whatever they like in school.'

The parents agreed, adding that it was very important the boys learned to respect the school.

There was a quiet knock on the door, and having been given permission to enter, Kamal and Amjad shuffled in, heads down, shoulders floppy, ready to be told off. They had a routine for this, which I'd witnessed on a number of occasions. They study the floor until told to look at someone, and then they make minimal eye contact, eyes rolling back to the floor as if they're made of lead, waiting to be told to apologise, when a muttered 'sorry' escapes barely moving lips. The routine is so practised I sometimes think it's an act, not something from the heart.

True to form, neither made any eye contact with anyone, and both examined the carpet while they waited for Chris to finish his recount of what happened earlier in the day. He then asked if either boy had anything to say.

Silence.

'Boys. Look at me. Look at me, Kamal. Look at me, Amjad.'

Their heads came up slowly. 'Sorry, sir' they mumbled, lips barely moving. As if the effort of apologising had exhausted them, their heads headed downwards, and they studied the floor again.

'Kamal, what are you doing?' his father asked. 'Why are you behaving like this?'

'Sorry dad.' Apology seemed to be the safest option at the moment.

'Christians are good people. It says in the Noble Quran that we must respect the people of the book.' Amjad's dad joined in. 'We must treat them with respect. *Isa* is one of our prophets.'

That is always one of the positives but also the challenges of Muslim-Christian relations. *Isa* (Jesus) is indeed a prophet in Islam, but the doctrines that are taught about *Isa* are different from the Christian understandings, especially when it comes to whether or not he is divine. For the moment, though, doctrinal scruples were of less relevance than the need to establish a common bond between everyone in the room.

'The people of the book are to be respected, do you understand?' Amjad's dad wasn't showing any mercy now.

'Yes dad. Sorry dad.' Amjad joined in with Kamal's strategy, mumbling his apology, with his eyes downcast.

Silence.

'There is one other thing.' Chris said.

The parents turned to look at him, enquiringly.

'Sometimes I have spoken with the boys, and I say to them, "Would you behave like this in the mosque?" and they always tell me "No." So then I ask them, "So why do you behave like this in school?" and they never have an answer for me.'

This question is one I've heard Chris and other teachers use a number of times. Especially when the boys misbehave, it seems to be the question of last resort, to try and get some sort of sense out of them. The mosque has a sacred standing, and all the children know that any sort of misbehaviour would not be tolerated there. Sadly, the same respect is not extended to school premises.

'So boys,' Chris asked, 'Look at me.'

Their downcast eyes turned up, two sullen faces stared at him.

'Well?' Chris asked. 'Would you behave like this in the mosque?'

Mr Hussain joined in. 'The mosque is a holy place. School is a holy place. They are the same, both are a holy place. You know how important the Prophet, peace be upon him, said that learning was. You must treat both places with the same respect Kamal. You must not behave like this.' The distress in his voice was clear as he struggled to find appropriate English words to express his disquiet with how his son had behaved.

Suddenly Amjad's mum joined in. This was the first time she'd spoken in English since she'd come into the entrance hall about twenty minutes previously. 'Amjad, Christian are good people. You not to do this.' A

53

finger jabbed for emphasis as she reverted to Somali for a more extended explanation of why such behaviour was inappropriate. Amjad looked upset, eyes to the ground. In response to a question, he spoke, briefly. Satisfied, his mother turned to Chris and said 'I am sorry for this behaviour. I tell him it must not happen again. He has said it will not.'

As Chris thanked her, I thought to myself, 'Chance would be a fine thing. I mean, I know the Prophet said "Paradise lies at the feet of mothers" and that mums are supposed to be incredibly important within Islam, but will he really do what he's told?' I'd seen these boys misbehave too often to believe that one sentence from mum was all that was needed to ensure perfect behaviour from now on. Maybe it would be enough, but I would reserve judgement for a few months.

It was the end of the school day, and with one final warning about their need to behave better, Chris sent the boys back to class to collect their things. He thanked the parents again, and they thanked him, asking him to make sure something was done to help the boys learn to behave themselves better. Chris assured them that it would, indicating that I would also be speaking with the boys' whole class, and agreeing that if needed, something more would be done next term. They also left.

'Well, that's all we can do really,' Chris said, coming back to his desk, having seen the parents out. He loosened his tie. 'I hate having to tell them off like that, but it's the only way.'

'Yeah, it is.' I concurred. 'There's nothing else we can do. Hopefully it will do some good. I bet those boys will be in trouble at home tonight. Did you see their parents' faces?'

'When?' Chris asked.

'When you told them about how they used "Christian" as an insult? They were definitely shocked. They weren't faking that. It was all for real. I'm sure of that. Wherever Kamal and Amjad are getting these ideas from, it's not from home.'

'So where is it then?' Chris asked.

'I dunno. It can't be the mosque. The one they go to is quite moderate really. And if it's not home, and not the mosque, then where is it?'

'Maybe each other I guess? That class don't really get on with each other, so maybe they're just winding each other up.' Chris stretched, and removed his tie completely, throwing it towards his bag. It just made it, landing in a semi-coiled pile half in, half out of the bag.

'Yeah, could be. I can't think of any other reason, that's for sure.' It seemed as likely an explanation as any to me.

'Like we've said before, we have to be hospitable to these kids, but we also have to help them learn where the boundaries are. Yes, we want to welcome them, to take good care of them, but that does not mean it's okay to insult Christians. They need to learn where the boundaries are. Oh well, there's nothing else we can do about it, just keep the boundaries clear.' Chris said. 'What're you doing tonight?'

'The usual. Teaching on the vicar training course. You?'

'I'm gonna have another look at the SEF, and then try and get away by six,' he said, stretching again.

'Don't stay too late. See you later. Cheers.'

'Thanks for today. See you later.' Chris opened his laptop, and started to type.

I glanced over at his face as he left. Lit by the screen, it had a slight glow. 'There's a man who is dedicated to his work,' I thought, as I headed out to collect my things and head for home.

Are you what you wear?

I didn't make it into St. Aidans at all on Thursday. My time was taken up with a funeral in the morning, and there were several planning meetings in the afternoon as we prepared for Christmas celebrations in church. I did have some time to visit the school on the Friday morning, and as I made my way to my office, I saw Karima, a Yemeni girl from year three sitting on the armchair outside the learning mentor's room. The big black leather chair was almost swallowing her up, and from the sullen look on her face, I don't think she'd have minded one little bit if it did.

I wished her a cheery good morning, but got only a muttered response. Wondering what had made her so upset, I dropped my bag and coat in my office, and went to the staff room to make a cup of tea. Tracy, the learning mentor, was making herself a drink.

'Morning, Tom,' she greeted me. 'Do you want tea? I'm just making myself one after clearing up from breakfast club.'

'That's be great. Thanks. Just milk please. I saw Karima sitting outside your room. Face like thunder. What's up with her? Shouldn't she be swimming with the rest of her class?' This was a special treat for the end of term, and a way of getting them ready for regular lessons next term.

'Well, that's just it. Her dad's said she can't go.'

'What? Why?' I was confused. Karima was talking to me only the week before about how she'd been swimming with her mum at the new pool, and how she'd really enjoyed it.

'She's not got the right costume.' Tracy said, handing me a mug.

'Thanks. What do you mean, her costume's not right?' I asked. What would a "wrong" swimming costume look like?

'She's only got a normal one, which she uses when she goes swimming with her mum. But that's a girls only session. Her dad's said that if it's mixed swimming then she needs an all-over suit, and she's not got one, so she can't go.'

'Oh right. And school don't do them, do they?'

'Nah. We don't sell swimming stuff. We're not a sports shop after all. We can lend them a normal costume, but if they want a special one, they've got to go and buy it themselves. There's plenty of places near here that sell them, so it's not that hard for them to go and get one if they want. I'll send a letter home with her, telling her where the best places are, and it'll be fine for next term. It's a shame she can't go today, but there was nothing we could do about it.

She turned up without a costume, we rang home to check if she could borrow a normal one, and dad said no. What can you do?'

'Nothing.' I agreed. 'That's a shame.'

'Still, I'll find her something nice to do, hopefully that'll cheer her up. I'd better go see her now.'

'Yeah, see you later.' I followed Tracy out of the room, still wondering about the whole issue of swimming. I've never been swimming with the school, but the staff tell me that some of the Muslim girls wear all in one, lycra figure-hugging suits. I don't quite see how this is that much more modest than a normal costume as it doesn't leave much to the imagination as far as body shape is concerned, but maybe it's the fact that the flesh isn't exposed to public view. I'm not completely sure why this should matter with a seven year old, but I guess it's about getting them ready for adult life.

Preparation for life as an adult Muslim is a complex area. If you ask a *mufti* or a *sheikh*, an Islamic scholar of some sort, he will probably tell you that puberty is the age of responsibility. By this they generally mean aged fourteen or so. I remember a discussion about fasting with some parents, and one said that as far as primary school age children went, 'We have for them exception. They try for one day, maybe two, then have a rest for one day, maybe two.' Fasting for the hours of daylight for thirty days is an extremely difficult thing to do, so no wonder eight year olds are not expected to fast for the whole time. This logic would also suggest to me that the swimming costume they wore would not matter either. But things are not that simple.

For some of the more conservative Muslim parents, it was important that their daughters learnt to dress modestly from a very young age, even if they had not yet learnt to fast.

By and large, clothing isn't really an issue in St. Aidans. The school is happy for girls to wear a headscarf or not, in accordance with parental wishes. The same is true in choice of swimming costume. There are occasional blips as parents attempt to align what they think their children should wear with what the school expects them to do, as this incident with Karima illustrates. But these are fairly minor, and no more of an issue than the perennial battle to persuade boys to come to school in smart black shoes not trainers.

The morning passed quickly as I wrote up the decisions our planning group had made the day before, allowing the Christmas Eve and Christmas Day services to take shape. Glancing out of the window at break time, I saw a clear illustration of how little clothing-related differences mattered in St. Aidans. Miriam, a Nigerian Pentecostal Christian girl in year six was holding hands with Aisha, a Yemeni Muslim girl in her class, who always wears a headscarf. They were walking happily and talking together, two friends with much more in common than the differences of race, religion and clothing that distinguished them. Naima, a Bangladeshi Muslim girl, was going over to join them.

Seeing Naima's bare head reminded me of a conversation I'd had with these three about headscarves several weeks before. The year six class is quite a small one: fourteen girls and just ten boys. Eleven of the girls are Muslims, and all except for Naima wear a headscarf. I was chatting with Miriam and Aisha about their class, and asked Miriam what she thought of the fact that most of the girls in her class wore a headscarf and she didn't. Her answer wasn't what I expected at all.

'Sometimes I feel left out, sir,' she said. 'When the other girls are all wearing one. I asked my mum about it, but she said that I shouldn't wear one.'

This answer was intriguing in itself, because I knew Miriam's mum as she was a parent governor. A large, loud, joyful Nigerian lady, she brought life and energy to our discussions in governors meetings, and she had never stuck me as the prohibitive type. Her clothing was always colourful and modest, and she always had a head covering of some sort herself. It wasn't as full as a Muslim one, but it certainly covered most of her hair.

'Why is that?' I asked Miriam. 'Your mother always wears some kind of a headscarf, doesn't she?'

'Yeah, but the school scarf is the Muslim one. I'm not allowed to wear it, because I'm a Christian.'

'Oh, I see. Do you mind?' I asked.

'Well, only a bit, sir. I understand why Mum doesn't want me to be Muslim. I mean, me and Aisha are friends, but our religion is different.'

'What do you think about that, Aisha?'

'It's fine, sir. Like Miriam said, we're friends even if our religion is different.'

'And what about wearing the headscarf? Do you like it?'

'Well sir, I've worn it since I was four. So I guess you could say that I really like it. But I do get really hot sometimes during PE.'

That I could well understand. At St. Aidans the school uniform headscarf was a single piece of cloth, almost like a hood that was pulled on over the head and moved into place. It covered the top of the head and down over the neck. If parents had opted to buy one their child could grow into, then there was often quite a lot of material bunched up around the neck. This meant the scarves were good at trapping heat. One or two of the girls "forgot" their headscarves when they were doing PE, although this was very much a minority strategy. The more common ploy was to untuck it, or to let it gradually slip back a bit, to let at least some of the heat escape. After PE on a hot summer's day—or even after a long hot summer's lunch time—it was common in St. Aidans to see the Somali and Yemeni girls in their headscarves, faces glowing or sometimes even dripping with sweat. While the extra warmth was welcome in the winter, in the summer it was the last thing they needed.

The tracksuit bottoms they wore for PE didn't help them keep cool either. The really interesting thing about PE kit was the difference in stance over what was expected for boys and girls. Technically the Islamic expectations of modesty and leg covering extend to both boys and girls, but in St. Aidans I'd only ever seen them observed for the girls. In summer all the boys wore just shorts, whether they were Muslim or not. But none of the girls ever did. Sometimes they'd wear shorts and leggings instead of tracksuit bottoms, partly because this was a bit cooler, and partly because it was more shapely, but they never exposed any flesh. Being a girl in St. Aidans was hot work in the summer months.

I'd asked some of the boys about this. Ahmed said it was fine to wear shorts, and even Kamal and Amjad, the *halal* police themselves, thought it wasn't a problem. But when I'd asked Aisha in year six I'd got a different point of view. She'd lived in the Yemen for most of the last year, and told me that 'the religious boys in Yemen would never wear shorts, because of *haya* (modesty).' She's certainly right that the Prophet never wore shorts, but then again he never wore trousers either. The link between clothing and religion can be complex, although at its heart, Muslims simply want to expose as little of their bodies as possible to the scrutiny of others.

There are two main strategies that Muslims tend to use when it comes to dressing modestly in accordance with Islamic expectations. Some go for a much more literalist strategy. This means men dress as closely as possible to the Prophet himself, down to wearing a silver ring on the little finger of the right hand, and dying their beards orange. Others go more for the spirit than the letter of the law, reasoning that any modest clothing is acceptable. Under this logic, a woman may not even need to cover her hair, and, provided she chose carefully, could dress in a very Western style.

'I'm sure you guys do get really hot in the summer, but I guess it keeps you warm in the winter. You must be glad of the extra warmth now.' I suggested to Aisha.

'Yeah sir, that's true. It does keep your ears warm when we're on yard now. And like I said, it's great if I've not had time to brush my hair in the morning as well.'

Now there was an advantage I'd not considered.

Fitting in is important when you're growing up, and the desire to conform shows itself in many different ways amongst school children, from Miriam's desire to wear a headscarf, to the boys' refusal to wear tracksuit bottoms for PE. No self-respecting boy would wear anything but shorts for a football match, and the Muslim lads in St. Aidans are no exception to this rule. In the social jungle of school, conformity is the camouflage many children choose to wear to survive.

Hafsa is a wonderful example of this. Every day she walks to school with her mum, dutifully wearing her school headscarf. But within minutes of getting into class, the headscarf is off her head, and in her bag, and her carefully plaited hair is on display for everyone to see. This doesn't bother her teacher one little bit. If she came to school in a non-uniform headscarf, then there would be trouble, but her decision to not wear one at all isn't a disciplinary matter, at least as far as the school's rules were concerned. And it's never been an issue with her classmates either. Maybe it's because she's not officially old enough to have to wear one, as the majority expectation is that the full demands of Islam aren't really applicable until one reaches puberty, and Hafsa is only nine.

Mind you, opinion varies. There's a Yemeni girl in the Reception class in the school who does wear a headscarf, just like Aisha had done, but none of the Bangladeshi girls do, whatever their age. They say you don't have to wear one till you go to high school. Another Yemeni girl told me she only wears hers when reading Quran or going to Arabic classes in the mosque. Many of the children seem to be quite skilled at this, adapting to the situation they're currently in, living multiple, parallel lives, always adapting, always doing their best to fit in, to be normal, which is just what all of us try to do. In a very real sense, what we wear does symbolise who we are, and the person most of us want to be is someone who is dressed to remain in a good relationship with those around about them.

No go zones

Friday afternoon is parents' knitting afternoon, or to be more accurate, mums' knitting afternoon. No dad that I know of is brave enough to enter such an oestrogen filled zone. This was the last one of term, so Tracy told me she was expecting quite a few of the mums to turn up, to finish off the different projects they'd been making. Aisha's mum's been making a hat apparently, and it keeps going wrong. She gets so excited chatting away with Tracy and the other mums that she keeps forgetting how many stitches to increase by and so she has had to keep starting again. It's the reknitted hat that's been made about five times, or so Tracy says. Apparently today's the day to finally finish it all off.

I did call in on the knitting once, but I'll never make that mistake again. The silence was quite brittle and the conversation froze so quickly you could've used the resultant ice to chill peas fresh from the field. Somali and Yemeni women really don't like strange men. I've learnt this, as with many lessons in life, through getting it wrong. It's all to do with family honour: they should only talk with men who are related to them, and, although this rule is relaxed for talking to teachers where necessary, at a social occasion like the knitting club it is as rigid as a wall of steel, and about as friendly. So on that one famous occasion, I quickly made my excuses and went on my way to do something else. I do sometimes ask Tracy how things are going, and she's keeping me posted on the continuing saga of the hat knitting, but that's about all I know of what's going on there.

Zumba is another thing I steer clear of, and not just because I've the rhythm and coordination of a giraffe on ice skates, but also because it's another high oestrogen, women only zone. The sessions run every Wednesday morning, free to mums (and aunties and so on)—part of St. Aidans service to the local community—helping promote fitness and a healthy lifestyle. Putting it on has been a real learning curve for the staff at St. Aidans, mainly about how to black out all the windows in a room, which is quite a shift in culture for a school. Following the Bichard enquiry into the murders of Holly Wells and Jessica Chapman, schools are really concerned with transparency and making sure everything is in public view. The safeguarding agenda is not just about keeping children safe from harm, but also about keeping every adult in school safe from malicious allegations. The best way to fulfill both of the agendas is to maximise the public nature of everything that goes on within the school. So every classroom door has a glass window in it, when staff work one-to-one with children doors are kept open and no one is ever hidden away from plain sight. So when the Yemeni and Somali mums all said they'd only come to Zumba if the windows were blacked out and the door was firmly kept shut throughout the session, it took some thinking about how to make that work.

Concealing any visitors to school, even Somali mums in black billowing *abiya* doesn't seem quite right to most staff, and as child protection governor, I could see what they meant. Schools do their best to avoid concealing anything, but in this case, we had to learn how to, because there was no way the Somali and Yemeni mums could do exercise in the level of clothing that modesty dictated they wear if men could see them. So John, the caretaker, fitted roller blinds to the doors of the dining room, and the vertical blinds on the windows were repaired, on the principle that blackout blinds and exercise were better than obesity and exposure. The side benefit was that if the school ever want to use that hall to show films, during a rainy break time for example, then they've got the perfect cinema set up.

But fitting the blinds was only one part of the solution; the harder part was to train all male members of staff—and indeed the boys—that when the blinds were down, that was a sign that this was now a female only zone. I've only forgotten twice, and the shouts of warning were enough to teach me what the blinds meant. Chris is a faster learner than me, and he only got it wrong once.

I knocked on his office door just after everyone had gone back to class for the afternoon's lessons. This was normally a quiet time, handy for having a more detailed discussion. I wanted to run through with him the plans for how Christmas would be celebrated in St. Aidans the following week. Chris had decided there wouldn't be a carol service this year, as it had taken up too much time to organise, and he was not especially keen on asking Muslim children to sing lots of Christmas carols. We'd agreed to have a Nativity play for Key Stage One, as everyone loves a cute child dressed as a sheep, and a Christingle service for the whole school, as everyone also loves free sweets, provided they're *halal*. What I wasn't sure of was whether I had some kind of a role in the nativity play. I was hoping not, and it turned out this wish was fulfilled.

Chris looked up as I came in. 'You okay?' he asked, stretching in his chair and rubbing his eyes.

'Good, thanks. Another early morning?' I moved a pile of papers from a chair and took a seat in his cluttered office.

'Yeah, 5:12am. It could've been worse. At least it was after five, which I'm counting as a positive.'

'It's always good to look on the bright side. I just wanted to check about the Nativity. Did you want me to do anything?' I asked.

Chris turned his head to one side as he thought for a moment. 'Nah, don't think so. I'll introduce and close. It's not really a service or anything is it?'

'No, I don't think so. It's mainly about the kids looking cute in their costumes, and granny being able to go "Ah, isn't she sweet", so there's not much point in me doing more than just being there.'

'True, but you're the main man for the Christingle. I'll leave all that to you, and just say thanks at the end and send the kids back to class and get the parents to wait till they can go and get them.'

'Sounds good to me.' I said, pleased that things were turning out as I'd hoped. 'Everything else okay?'

'Yeah, it's all fine. I do need to tell you something as child protection governor though.'

'What's that?' Sadly in a school such as St. Aidans, with such high mobility and so many needy parents and pupils, child protection issues were all too common. Although in some schools the child protection governor gets told about every single incident, there were too many of them for me to be kept up to date with the details of each one, and so for Chris to tell me something, it had to be a serious incident. Turned out it was more that he needed a sounding board, and I was the first suitable one that he encountered.

Chris wanted to know whether I thought he needed to call Childline. He'd just finished meeting with another parent. Hamza was a boy in year six; his dad had been called in because Hamza had kicked Tracy at the end of breakfast club when she'd told him to stop his game of pool and pack up because it was time to go on yard. Hamza is a sulky Somali lad, who's had one of those growth spurts eleven year old boys sometimes have, and he's not quite aware of how big and strong he's becoming.

Chris said he didn't think Hamza actually meant to kick Tracy at all hard, but had simply swiped in her general direction because although he's big, he has the emotional control of a toddler at times, and thinks with his feet and fists more than with his head. But even if it was unintentional, an assault on a member of staff couldn't go unpunished, and so Hamza's dad was called in for Chris to explain why Hamza would be suspended for two days. We don't like punishments like suspension in St. Aidans, thinking of them as more of a defeat than anything else, as it's a sign we've not be able to care for a child properly. But we do also believe in the importance of good discipline, clear boundaries, and that all actions have consequences. Regrettably this means that at times like this suspension is the only course of action available.

That much was unremarkable, but it was what happened next that caused Chris concern. Hamza and his dad were sitting next to each other in Chris' office while all this was explained. As soon as he heard his son was suspended from school for two days, Hamza's dad had turned to him, called him a 'stupid boy' and clipped him over the head with the hand that was also holding his mobile phone. He hit his son so hard that the cover came off the phone.

'So do you think that counts as assault?' Chris wanted to know. 'I think it does, but they only came in after lunch, and I'm still working out what to do.'

'I reckon it does.' I said.

'I was shocked at the time,' Chris continued, 'I said to him "You can't do that" and he just looked at me and said, "I can. He is my son. I will discipline him as I please." And he pulled Hamza to his feet by his ear, and marched him out of here, dragging him by the ear. They've just gone about half an hour ago.'

'Well, that settles it. I'm sure you need to report that. Childline can decide what to do about it.'

'You're right.' Chris reached for his phone, and pressed the button for the office. 'Barbara' he said, 'It's only me. Have you got an address for Hamza Sherif in year six? Thanks.'

He hung up, and said, 'Thanks for that.'

'Pleasure. I'll leave you to it.'

As I turned to leave, the phone buzzed. Chris picked it up, 'Hi. 32 Waldgrave Avenue. Thanks Barbara.'

I closed the door, and headed back to my own office, thinking about how often such phone calls to Childline had to be made. The sad thing was that they were quite frequent, and Hamza's dad would probably get a visit from either the police or the social workers by the end of the day. The question was, whether anything else would happen after that.

Probably, if Hamza was asked if he wanted to make a complaint, he'd say no. Certainly that was what had happened the past few times anyone had that option. The Somali community that was linked to St. Aidans was incredibly close-knit, of a dense weave that virtually nothing could penetrate, certainly not an enquiring white-British policeman. Somali men were clear they had the right to physically discipline their children, and neither their children nor their wives disagreed with them.

It was just the same with other stuff that may—or may not—have been going on. Culturally, it was expected that Somali girls would undergo female circumcision when they were nearing puberty. This is something I'd never been able to understand: why anyone thought it was a good idea to cut off the external parts of a woman's genitalia and sew up her vagina is completely beyond me. I have heard the argument that it was cultural, and I could understand the idea that it was about protecting a woman's honour, and even sort of comprehend those who said it empowered women because it gave them greater control over their sexuality. But when you got down to it, the whole idea was just something that made me feel uncomfortable. I can't see how it is honouring to God or your family, really. Being a white man, and a Christian minister to boot, it wasn't an issue I'd ever had to deal with in my work at St. Aidans. Indeed as far as I'm aware, none of the staff had ever encountered it. But I still wondered about whether it was going on. Certainly, the articles I'd read from medical staff based in Tower Hamlets and other areas with a high Somali population suggested that it was common practice throughout the UK, so I saw no reason to assume it wasn't going on here as well. There is nothing in the Quran that explicitly comands this practice, and so it is arguably more about Somali culture than Islamic teaching, but when over ninety-nine per cent of Somalis are Muslims, the line between culture and religion becomes so fuzzy that it ceases to exist. For some Muslims at least, female circumcision was an expected norm.

The other unspoken problem was about domestic violence. This concerned the Bangladeshi community, and perhaps other communities as well. Chris once told me that he thought every single Bangladeshi family that had some kind of a connection to St. Aidans was in some way affected by domestic violence. But none of the families ever split up over it. At least not permanently. Mum and the kids might go and stay with a cousin or granny for a few days, but that was as far as it went. Which meant there was nothing that we could actually do to deal with the problem. I think that the staff at St. Aidans are highly skilled at sensitively tackling difficult issues, but you can't begin to try and solve a problem until everyone admits there is something that needs to be dealt with. While people pretend everything in the garden is lovely, should you let them continue to do so?

Problems in the shadows are by far the hardest to tackle. Kamal and Amjad's fight was clearly wrong, and could be tackled firmly and swiftly. But Hamza's dad presented an entirely different challenge, one that was much more complex. He was undisputed head of his family, but that did not make his behaviour acceptable or right. How could it be challenged, and how could the school work with his sons to stop them growing up thinking they should behave in the same way?

Another tricky subject was different expectations of gender roles. If Muslim women are taught that any form of conversation with an unrelated man brings shame and dishonour on their family, then how exactly do they attend a parents' evening if the teachers they need to visit are male? Moreover, if they did not speak much English, how would they talk with the teacher if they did manage to attend? Bringing up the children was their responsibility in their family, but if they could not communicate with the school staff, it would be very tricky indeed. Running a Christian school in a multi-cultural, multi-faith area is very complicated, and demands a degree of sophistication and sensitivity that is not always acknowledged. We learn to work both in public and also in the shadows of the no-go zones.

The cutest child?

The weekend was busy, as you might expect in the run up to Christmas. Saturday was my day off, which meant I spent most of the time shopping, writing Christmas cards and so on. We had our Sunday School nativity on Sunday morning. This was the usual chaos of small children forgetting their lines or wandering off the stage at precisely the wrong moment. Such services make for a great spectator sport—whether you're playing 'spot the cutest costume,' 'spot the most embarrassing mistake,' or even 'spot the attempt to make a fool of the vicar,' there's plenty of fun for all the family. Monday morning brought a variation on this theme, with the St. Aidans nativity play dress rehearsal.

Generally the older children really enjoy watching it, although the run up to Christmas itself can sometimes cause them a few problems. This surprised me, because I'd thought that Easter would be more of a problem for Muslims than Christmas, but in St. Aidans at least, this isn't the case. I had a chat about this with Miriam and Aisha in year six, asking them which they thought would be more of a problem for a Muslim, Christmas or Easter.

Miriam spoke first, 'Oh definitely Easter, sir, because it's when he rose.' The Nigerian Pentecostal girl's faith wasn't just a label for the census form. It was a living reality. She goes to church every Sunday, for most of the day by all accounts, and is involved with a couple of clubs during the week as well.

Miriam's views on the greater problem Easter would pose for a Muslim had been exactly what I'd been thinking as well. The Christian celebration of the death and resurrection of Jesus, doctrines the Quran specifically denies, would surely be the flash point and greatest source of conflict between Christians and Muslims. There is much closer agreement about Christmas. Admittedly the Quran does not say Jesus was the Son of God, but *surah Maryam*, the chapter that describes Jesus' birth, does teach that John was born to Zechariah and his wife in their old age, and that Mary was a virgin when she gave birth to Jesus, and that he was a servant of Allah and a prophet. Much common ground, suggesting to me that Christmas would be far less of a problem to a Muslim than Easter. But both Miriam and I had made the same mistake in our reasoning—we'd assumed that doctrinal religion was more important than lived religion. However, that is precisely wrong. It turns out that what bothers people more is not what those around them believe, but what they do.

When you think about this in more detail, it does make good sense. Suppose you and I are good friends. As far as I'm concerned, if your faith is just an intellectual thing, then you can believe whatever you like: that the earth is flat, the moon is made of cheese, there is a huge mountain far to the north of here on which the gods live, or any one of a number of religious beliefs. So long as you simply hold those beliefs in your head, and don't do anything that impacts my life, I can still be friends with you, and your beliefs will have little impact on our friendship. But as soon as your lived religion starts to impact my life, then there is all sorts of potential to conflict. So if your belief that the moon is made of cheese means I can no longer eat lasagne, then we've got a problem. And this was precisely the point that Aisha identified.

'No, sir,' she said firmly. 'It's Christmas. Easter doesn't really bother us in school. I just say *stafallah* when you say stuff I don't believe in assembly. And besides, we get free chocolate, and I like the eggs. But Christmas is harder.'

When I thought about it a bit more, I could understand why Easter might not have been much of a problem. After all, even though St. Aidans was a Church of England school, Easter wasn't a major feature of the school's calendar. Granted they learnt about the Christian view of Easter in RE, but then they also learnt about the founding of Sikhism and what Buddhists believed, and neither of those posed a major problem to being a Muslim in Britain. And for Aisha and her friends, there were only two very brief times in the school year when they encountered Easter. One was an assembly on a Monday morning, taken by me, which was much like any other assembly, and the other was a free chocolate egg to take home on the last day of the spring term. So all in all, despite the fact that Muslims may not be in doctrinal agreement with Christians over Easter, there is some logic to the idea that the lived religion of Christmas is in fact harder for Muslims to deal with, at least in a school context.

When I questioned Aisha as to why Christmas was harder, she wasn't so sure. She didn't mind Christmas decorations particularly; indeed she quite liked the tree with the pretty lights. She even gave cards wishing her friends 'Seasons greetings' and she also gave a present to both Mrs Morgan, her teacher, and Miss Williams, the teaching assistant in her class. It seemed it was more of a cumulative thing, simply the piling up of layer upon layer of cultural and confessional Christian baggage that was a bit of a weight to carry. Christmas, although it was fun, was also hard work.

And such exclusion was difficult to resist simply by staying *stafallah*. This Arabic phrase, an abbreviation of *astaghfirullah*, means 'May Allah forgive me.' Normally it's said when, as Aisha put it, 'you've done something naughty,' but it is also sometimes said in an almost talismanic sense when one has just heard something blasphemous, and was a popular phrase in St. Aidans. This usage is almost instinctive, one of many Arabic phrases that children brought up in Muslim households use, almost entirely without thinking. *Insha'Allah* (if God wills it) is another, as in 'I'll see you tomorrow *insha'Allah.*' The speaker may well not think God is especially involved in determining whether she sees you tomorrow, but then neither is an Austrian that concerned about the divine view on something when she says *grüß Gott* in greeting. Such phrases pepper the speech of many countries, and I could no more assume that Aisha's *stafallah* is any more religious than Helen's 'Bless you' said after I sneezed.

All of this meant I had to think carefully about what Aisha was doing when she said *stafallah* in one of my Easter assemblies. It is possible that when I talked about Jesus dying on a cross, she simply said '*stafallah*,' to indicate her disagreement and invoke protection against Allah's displeasure at hearing such a blasphemy. But she may have said it entirely instinctively, in response to something she knew she disagreed with; I wouldn't want to over-analyse exactly what she was doing. What's more, I have to admit that if she hadn't told me she said *stafallah* at such times, then I would have had no idea she was saying it, and I'm still unsure how many other pupils might also be saying it, not that it was any of my business. This is why it's so effective a response: it allows Muslim pupils to resist assemblies and other places where they encounter confessional Christianity without having to resort to a more overtly confrontational approach. All they do is disagree with a doctrine, and since the focus of the assembly isn't really on lived religion (no one is asking them to do anything specifically Christian after all), no one gets upset. For the few who want to say it, *'stafallah'* thus becomes a means towards peaceful coexistence, not a point of contention.

Mind you, I doubt anyone would have said *stafallah* at the nativity play. As I said before I got distracted, Monday was the dress rehearsal, which meant that the older children got to come and watch their younger siblings try and remember their lines and cues in front of an audience. It was a really successful performance. By the time I got to the hall, the older children were already sitting expectantly, whispering to each other in anticipation of what was to come. The performers filed in, in the main looking quite keen to be there, but a few looking hesitant and slightly unsure about the whole idea of having to speak in front of other people. The older children started to crane their necks, and nudge their neighbours as they spotted their brothers and sisters looking slightly cute and slightly embarrassed at having to dress as a sheep or a camel or a star.

During the performance itself, the atmosphere was wonderful: friendly, warm and just like a family having fun together. The children sang-shouted their lines almost perfectly in time with the CD, and the teaching assistant in charge of the laptop managed to get the slides to transition in near perfect time. There were a couple of amusing incidents: the second king to speak elbowed his predecessor out of the way slightly too violently in his haste to get to the microphone, the stars' dance with glowsticks was lovely, but got slightly out of sync towards the end and one of the sheep fell asleep and so missed her cue to come on stage. Apparently she always falls asleep during the songs, which she thinks of as lullabies, so there was nothing new there. All these were just minor teething issues that could soon be sorted out. The rest of the school loved it. Year five and six wouldn't sit still. They kept standing up to point out their siblings and to laugh at children looking distressingly cute in sheep costumes.

Once they were finished, Chris told them how well they'd done, and sent the younger children back to their classes to get changed and the older children back to their classes to do some more Christmas craft and activities. I thanked Richard, the Early Years manager, and told him what a fantastic job he had done of it all. Heading back over to my office, I bumped into Fiona Williams, the year six teaching assistant.

'That was great, wasn't it?' I said 'Year six looked like they were really enjoying it.'

'They did once we got them there,' she replied with a wry smile.

That sounded intriguing, so I enquired further, and she explained. Apparently several of the boys were convinced that watching a nativity play was *haram* because it was Christian, and therefore were very sulky about the idea of going. They're the kind of boys who can swing a crowd with their vocally expressed opposition, older versions of Kamal and Amjad really, with more practice at being awkward, so this could have caused a real problem. Fortunately Fiona thinks quickly on her feet, and pointed out to these boys that since the story of the virgin birth of Jesus is actually in the Quran, this didn't really make much sense. They were initially sceptical, but she has a copy of the Quran on her phone, and so she found *surah Maryam*, read it to them, and they realised that their argument didn't really have much weight at all, and so their opposition wilted and died.

'They can get a bit upset and combatative at times, those lads, can't they?' I concluded.

'They certainly can. Make me wonder what they will make of the Christingle.' Fiona added.

'Well, indeed. They were okay with it last year, I think. Probably because they got free sweets.'

'Yeah, it's amazing what a difference a free sweet makes. What was really interesting, though, was that they had no idea those verses were in the Quran. I think I freaked them out a bit, because I knew a bit of their holy book that they didn't.'

'Yeah, I can see how that would be a problem,' I smiled. 'But it's quite common I think. Many of them are probably learning classical Arabic, and can probably read a fair amount. But they don't learn how to translate it. They simply memorise the text. I've met some Muslims who are good at translating the Quran, but plenty of them just memorise sections, even the entire thing, without worrying about translating it.'

'Gosh, that's really different from Christianity, isn't it?' Fiona commented. 'Christians are really into translating the Bible and so on, aren't them. I'm glad of that—wouldn't want to have to learn Greek and Hebrew, as I'm rubbish at languages.'

'I know what you mean. One of the challenges for St. Aidans is, I think, to help the Muslim pupils understand the teachings of their own faith about engaging with others. There's no point in us just teaching in RE that Christians think we should love our neighbours—we need to look for examples in the history of Islam where it happens as well.'

'I guess so,' said Fiona. 'See you later, need to get back to class,'

Having successfully escaped my nascent sermon before it went into full flow, Fiona headed off. She had recognised one of my hobbyhorses. As with any religion, there are some incidents with the history of Islam where hospitality was definitely not shown to those of other faiths. There are sadly many Muslim majority countries in the world today where to be a Christian is to risk death. But there are some occasions in history where Muslims did care for and welcome everyone. Many Muslims turn to the example of the tenth century caliphate in Cordoba, Spain as a shining example of a Muslim ruled state where Christians and Jews were welcomed and encouraged to participate fully in society.

Muslims in Britain like to refer to Abdullah Quilliam, a high profile convert to Islam at the end of the nineteenth century, who was a generous philanthropist. There are plenty of models for positive engagement, if we only look for them.

The parents certainly didn't think that the nativity play was *haram* at all. They came out in great numbers the following afternoon, not all on time and not always quietly, but they came. Virtually every one had a phone or camera to film the play on, and most of them seemed to concentrate on that, almost to the point where they didn't actually engage emotionally with the play at all. I positioned myself at the very back of the hall, initially holding the door to let parents maneuver their tank-like buggies into the hall, and then later relegated to a light switch to dim the lights for the stars' dance. At one point when everyone was singing a song about the shepherds coming to Bethlehem I glanced at the Yemeni gentleman on my left, his face expressionless as he concentrated on the screen of his phone and capturing his daughter's every move. The Somali man standing next to him had the same glazed expression, although in his case it was his son's singing he was focused on filming. The parents on my right were just the same. This really was a performance, in every sense of the word.

There really wasn't any religion in the school nativity play, which I guess is why it wasn't really a problem for any of the parents to watch it or for the children to join in with it. The underlying theme may be a religious one, but there was no way anyone could describe this as confessional worship. It was simply the children putting on a show for their parents to enjoy, or at least to film and put on Facebook. There are a whole bunch of child protection issues that all this raised, but I decided that at present it really wasn't worth going there with any of them. Maybe it's a cop-out, but with so many other challenges at the moment, it didn't seem like a good time.

Drip feeding

Now that I think about it, agreeing to do an RE lesson with year four on the last Wednesday of term was probably a mistake. But as they say, I learnt so much from my last mistake, I think I'll make another one. Hopefully this mistake will be a worthwhile one and at least someone will benefit from it. I'd agreed with Chris last week that I'd come and talk with year four about how it was possible to be a Muslim in a Christian school, and it was time to fulfill that promise.

The Messenger is a perfect film for this situation. It tells the story of the foundation of Islam. I always find it an interesting viewing experience because in accordance with Muslim reverence for the Prophet, he is never shown on screen, and so characters often talk directly to the camera and respond as if someone has spoken when the viewers hear no sound at all. Fortunately these issues were not relevant for the portion I'd decided to use.

I'd agreed with Phil, the year four teacher, that I'd show a short clip from the film and then we'd talk about exactly what it had to teach them about how they should get on with each other in St. Aidans. I showed the occasion of the first *hijrah*, the first journey that the Muslims made from Mecca to Abyssinia, modern day Ethiopia. The Muslims were experiencing persecution in Mecca, and so some fled, looking for a safer place to live. They came to Abyssinia, and pleaded with the Christian king, the Negus, to allow them to stay. He was initially quite welcoming, but then a delegation came from Mecca to request the return of these runaway slaves and religious rebels, as they termed them. On learning it was a religious dispute and that some of the men were free, the Negus summoned both sides in the argument in order to sit in judgement in the case.

This was the clip from *The Messenger* that I'd decided to show year four, because I hoped the judgement reached would be one that would speak into their situation in St. Aidans. I told them to watch it and think about what this had to say to their experience of school, and that we'd talk about it once we'd finished watching. I think the clip was perfect. The leader of the Meccan delegation gave a masterclass in arrogant distain. Every time he was rude about Mohammed, several of the Muslim boys muttered '*stafallah*' spontaneously under their breath as they watched. The Negus was suitably regal and majestic, and his final judgement was just the opener I needed.

In the clip, the Meccan delegate does his best to get the Muslims condemned as heretics by saying they deny the divinity of Jesus. The Negus, learning of the possibility of heretical views of Jesus rounds on them demanding, 'Speak to me of Christ. Speak of Christ.' It's a tense moment. Will the Muslims compromise in their beliefs to procure safety?

Will their uncompromising stance lead to their death, either at the hands of the Negus or in their return to Mecca? What would happen to these refugees?

The Muslim spokesman responds without fear. 'I will recount the exact words. We say what our Prophet has taught us: he is God's servant, His messenger, His Spirit, His Word that He breathed into Mary, the Holy Virgin.' The Meccan is sure they are now condemned, exclaiming triumphantly, 'But not the Son, not the Son.' However, this is sufficient for the Negus, who stood, drew a short line in the sand and said, 'The difference between you and us does not exceed the length of this line,' granting the Muslims the peace and security they were seeking.

Personally, I think the difference between the Muslim and Christian understanding of Jesus is greater than the line the Negus drew, since I regard the Muslim denial of the divinity of Christ as a point which requires serious dialogue and discussion. Be that as it may, the Negus represented a different view, one that was useful in this particular situation. As I explained to the class, he stood firm, welcomed the Muslims, and they lived in harmony together with their Christian hosts, neither side forcing their beliefs on the other. The relationship was so cordial that some of the Muslims stayed there for the rest of their lives, even when Islam was under threat during the battles of Badr and Uhud.

This clip lasted for about ten minutes, and as the children watched it I watched them. Kamal and Amjad were amongst those who said *stafallah* when the Prophet was insulted. Agnieska and Helenka, two recent arrivals from Poland, watched in slightly bemused puzzlement, foreheads wrinkled as they tried to work out what this had to do with them and their experience of school. The only time I'd ever talked to them about the Somali presence in the school, they'd talked about the 'black people' and how they 'believed different things from us.' I think this was probably more because their English isn't very good than because they're racist, but it was a salutary reminder that just because you're in the same class as someone, it doesn't mean to say you necessarily know much about them. Many of the other children sat with their chins cupped in their hands, happy enough to watch a film as a better alternative to writing.

Once the film clip was finished, I asked them what they thought about the clip. We began by recapping what the clip had covered, before moving on to discuss what it might mean for life in St. Aidans. We got there in the end, but it did take quite a while. Scott suggested that it meant all religions were the same, but several others disagreed with him. Ahmed talked about how it taught that we should respect people regardless of religion, that we should learn to understand each other and so on. This was my cue to talk a bit about how important respecting difference was, and how it was a key part of growing up. I also singled out the particular point that using one religion to insult another was definitely wrong. I decided to bite the bullet and specifically mention the use of 'Christian' as an insult, although I didn't name names. I talked about how upsetting it was for something very important to me personally, my Christian faith, to be used as a means of insulting others. Some of the more empathetic children did understand what I meant, but the furrowed brows of a few of them suggested to me that there was still work to be done in helping some of the class make the necessary emotional leap to see the world from a different point of view.

Phil finished off the discussion by talking again about the problems of discrimination: he picked out in particular the sexism of some of the boys, and challenged that as well, saying that this attitude was also unacceptable. The Meccan delegate in the film clip we'd watched had been incredibly sexist, describing women as commodities to buy and sell, not people to love. One or two of the boys had sniggered appreciatively at his comments, and Phil wanted them to know exactly how wrong he thought this attitude was. The sad thing was that it had been some Muslim lads who were being sexist, which is ironic given that one point that *The Messenger* tries to make is how Islam brought in an era of more positive treatment of women compared to that which preceded it. Unfortunately, sexism is another issue that lurks below the surface of some of the boys' behaviour, and the staff at St. Aidans also it challenge whenever possible.

Once the children had all gone out for break, I thanked Phil for letting me speak to them and he said, somewhat cynically, that it was not going to make that much of a difference because they were still going to behave in an unacceptable fashion to each other. Not that this meant it wasn't worth doing, he added, but that it was important to be realistic as to what can be achieved in such a short space of time. The fact that we've told the class Islam teaches respect for others doesn't mean to say they will actually respect others, he explained.

Phil also mentioned a conversation he'd had with Ahmed, a Somali member of staff, about how the children in Somalia are taught to hit back when they are hit, which stands in marked contrast with the 'turn the other cheek' teaching enshrined in Christianity. This didn't entirely surprise me: at its heart there probably is a fundamental difference in how Islam reacts to persecution, since once the Muslims were in Medina, war became an option for Mohammed and his followers, which it never was for Jesus and his disciples. If the difference between Islam and Christianity is this fundamental, I wondered, does it mean that potentially there is nothing to be done, and that Muslim children will always be more aggressive than Christian children?

That did seem an overly negative view. This current year four class is far more confrontational than any other I've known. All the classes in St. Aidans also have quite a few Muslim children in them and none of the other classes seem to have these problems, so it's probably just this particular group. Phil said that a few weeks ago he'd talked with them about all kinds of discrimination and about how wrong that was, but here we were again dealing with the same issues. He and I continued to chat about this and concluded that the only solution was to take a drip, drip approach, and that the more different ways the same message about getting on with each other was put across, the more likely it was to have some sort of an impact.

This was the thinking behind my ideas about the school as a Christian body, another lesson I was hoping to take with this class sometime. If you read the apostle Paul's teaching about the body of Christ in 1 Corinthians 12, it soon becomes clear that he is playing with a popular image from his day. Paul's contemporaries used the metaphor of a group of people as a body to maintain the status quo:

the poor peasants were the arms and legs that had to work hard to provide food for the stomach. Since the stomach did ultimately provide nutrition for the whole body, its apparent idleness was essential for the welfare of all. Bizarre logic, but it apparently convinced some people.

Paul uses the idea of a body in a radically different way. He suggests that the weaker parts (by which he means the genitals, though I bet you've never heard it said in church) are essential for the proper functioning of the body. This means that for a Christian body to be a Christian body, it needs weaker people, who are entirely dependent on others, since to be a Christian means to care for those who cannot care for themselves. I demonstrate the reality of my faith, after all, by my ability to love others in practical, concrete ways. For a school context, this means those who are more able must spend extra time and energy helping those who are less able, a great lesson for all of us to learn.

As I explained to Phil, it was about moving beyond tolerance towards respect, demonstrated in action. Tolerance isn't, in my view, a virtue to be promoted, so much as a foothill to climb beyond. That's to say, faced with mutual dislike and aggression, it's better to be tolerant than to hate, but it's far, far more preferable to respect than merely to tolerate. That's because tolerance assumes there's still a problem—something that's allowed to fester for the moment but that maybe we'll deal with later on—whereas respect recognises the validity of the other point of view, and engages with difference on an equal footing, rather than assuming the posture of superiority or paternalism that comes with tolerance.

Year four got a chance to have a go at respecting difference that afternoon when we had our school Christingle assembly.

For me this involved quite a long time spent with oranges. Barbara in the office had been very kind and put red electrical tape around them all, and had put the *halal* sweets on the cocktail sticks. Tracy and I then sat for a few hours putting the candles into the top of the oranges and stabbing four cocktail sticks into each orange.

Parents had also been invited to come along, and quite a few did. They sat in the middle of the hall on chairs, and the children surrounded them, some of the youngest sitting on chairs in front of them, and the older ones on chairs, mats and benches all around them. Years five and six sat together with the children from the nursery and reception, partly to help them sit and concentrate, and partly to distract them from wanting to play with the candles themselves.

I think one of the reasons why most of the Muslim pupils don't really have an issue with the Christingle assembly is that it's really difficult to build a clear, strong connection between a Christingle and Christianity. They do have to sing two Christmas songs, one at the start and one at the end of the assembly. This is an issue for some of them, as there's no tradition of singing songs in Islamic worship, and opinion is divided amongst the community as to whether music itself is permitted. All this makes singing quite an interesting challenge. It's certainly true that Muslim pupils never seem completely happy when there's a Christian song of any sort, which is hardly surprising, but in this case they made a reasonable effort at singing the carols, sing-shouting with some enthusiasm.

My technical explanation of the Christingle's symbolism seemed to work okay: some of the teachers must have talked their classes through what it meant before they came, because years three and five could all put up their hands and tell me that the orange symbolised the world, the sweets on sticks the good gifts of creation, the red tape the blood of Jesus and the candle the idea of Jesus as light of the world. The short video I showed of some children acting out the nativity story worked very well as a recap of what Christmas is all about, and the moment when we lit all the Christingle candles was great.

There is something about candlelight that has a wonderfully calming—even spiritual—effect on people of all ages, and today was no exception. The youngest children had been told to hold their oranges very carefully and they all did, the flickering of the candle flames reflecting in their eyes, pupils dilated because of the lack of light, as they stared in fascination at the candle each one held. Even the older children were transfixed, and I wondered exactly how many of them were listening as I told them to think about all the good things they'd enjoyed over the past year, and then to join with me if they wanted to in a short prayer thanking God for his goodness and kindness to each of us over the past year. The heads of many of the parents were bowed at this point. I've no way of knowing whether they were praying in their own way (Islam does have a tradition of *du'aah,* spontaneous prayer, as well as the set pattern of *salat*) or simply showing respect. Whichever it was, it encouraged me.

My biggest surprise came right at the end of the assembly. I finished with a prayer of blessing, which I don't normally do, but on this particular occasion it seemed like a good plan. In the prayer I thanked God again for his goodness and asked him to watch over the children and their families.

After Chris had sent the children back to class, a Somali lady in a black *abiya* came up to me and thanked me for the prayer. '*Salaam aleikum.* Thank you father for blessing our family' she said.

'*Wa aleikum salaam.*' I replied, 'God's blessing be upon you as well.'

With that she left, heading out of the hall to collect her children. I'd never spoken to her before, and probably never will again. But we shared this moment of peace, and that was enough for me. For many of the children, probably the best moment of the whole Christingle assembly was when they discovered that the sweets were *halal* and so they could eat them. For me it was this reminder that even if some of the children find it difficult to get on with each other in this Christian environment, at least some of their parents actively want to engage with the Christianity they encounter there.

What Christmas means to me

Thursday was the last full day of term, and I thought I would chat with some of the children about Christmas. Having spoken yesterday with year four about their behaviour, it didn't seem appropriate to go back today, and so I decided that I'd call in on year five instead. Their teacher, Becca, loves having visitors in the afternoon, especially this close to the end of term, when no real work is getting done. A chat about Christmas and what it means to me would be just the thing: it's work without really being work, just what they needed to fill in the final hours of the last full day of term.

For me, Christmas is a complex mix. There are some painful memories: my dad went into hospital just before Christmas when I was seventeen, and he never came out, dying the following January. Every Christmas since then has been tainted by these memories. I told them about this, not to make them upset, but simply to point out that

Christmas isn't always a happy, fun occasion for everyone, even for Christian ministers. I spared them the details, simply explaining that when I was younger my dad had been in hospital over Christmas, and even now when I think of Christmas parties I remember not really enjoying them because I was worried about my dad. I also added in a comment about the challenge of materialism; that happiness doesn't just come from getting more stuff, an idea that they found quite hard to deal with, especially those who had long lists of presents they were hoping for. I also emphasised the positive: the fun of seeing your family and in particular how special it is for me to be able to celebrate the birth of Jesus with my biological and my Christian family.

I asked them what Christmas meant to them, and they gave a real range of answers, from the positive to the negative. For many of the Muslim children, 'boring' was the most apposite description. Everywhere is shut, there is no particular reason for their families to gather, and so they end up just sitting around at home with little or nothing to do, wishing counter-intuitively that school was still open. They were also a bit confused about what to believe about Christmas. Several of them stated quite firmly that they didn't believe any of the Christian ideas about Christmas, but that Easter was okay with them. I read to them from *surah Maryam*, which is the Quranic passage that describes the Muslim understanding of the Virgin Mary and the circumstances around Jesus' birth. I didn't tell them where it was from, but simply asked them at the end what book they thought it was from. Without exception they all settled on the Bible, and were genuinely surprised when I corrected them. They got particularly excited looking at the Quranic Arabic and its English interpretation on my phone, and one or two proudly managed to read me a few sentences of the Arabic, which I had to assume were accurately pronounced. What was interesting was that although they could read the words, the children struggled to translate it into English. This reflects the priority put on Quranic memorisation within Islam. For many Muslims it is more important to have learnt the words that to be able to translate them all. Once a few of them had been able to read the text, I asked them if any of them found Christmas difficult, and most did not, but some suggested that, as with Aisha, the fact that there was so much Christmas stuff going on, in the shops as well as in school, for such a long time that it did eventually get a bit exhausting.

I talked with Becca once the children had gone out for afternoon break, and she confirmed this same feeling; Christmas is so omnipresent that it wears the Muslim children out after a while. We were still talking about this as we walked to the staffroom to make a cup of tea, and Phil heard us as we all stood by the kettle waiting for it to boil.

'I'm sure that's what got to Kamal,' he said.

'What do you mean?' Becca asked.

'Well, when we got back from the Christingle yesterday, he put his on the desk, refused to eat the sweets, and just poked at the orange trying to move it as far away from himself as possible. I asked him why and he said he didn't want to touch it. And he wasn't prepared to believe that the sweets were *halal*, so he ended up just leaving the whole thing behind at the end of the day.'

We continued chatting about how most of the children get on fine with being in St. Aidans, and indeed, as Becca put it, 'they're privileged to be learning together with such a diverse group of friends.' But just a few of them really struggle and maybe, as Phil suggested, 'all we can do is help them to contain it, or at least help them to learn not to express their unease quite so vocally.'

'I'm sure you're right, but we do need to try and help them expand their boundaries—you know, like with that church visit, Phil.'

'Yeah, that was definitely an exercise in expanding comfort zones.'

As part of their RE module on Christian places of worship, Phil had asked me to organise a tour of church for his class. I'd done this sort of thing many times before, and usually quite enjoyed it. You can make them quite fun for kids, getting out the different pieces of silverware, giving them communion wafers to taste, the microphones to try out and so on. But on this particular occasion, we first had to persuade the kids it was okay for them to even go into the church building. For some reason Kamal and Amjad, the perennial troublemakers, decided that even entering a church building was *haram* and said they had to go to the nursery instead while the rest of the class went on the visit.

Phil had mentioned this to me. When I asked why it was the nursery, he said that was because Kamal and Amjad were looking for the easiest option. 'It's not about religion at all. They just don't want to go.' Before we went out, we had to tell the boys that this was an educational trip, there would be no Christian prayers, (the thing they were really concerned about) and their parents were quite happy for them to go.

We eventually persuaded them to go, and as it turned out, they really enjoyed it. The boys just don't like trying anything new, but when they are comfortable in a new situation they're quite happy. They enjoyed trying the communion wafers and were both fascinated and horrified by the dead spider that Amjad spotted in the church baptistry.

'They'll not forget that spider in a hurry.' Phil said. 'It's a bit like your assemblies. They may say that they don't like Christianity, and it's true that sometimes they're a bit uncomfortable with prayers and that, but they still love watching the cartoons or the activities, especially if there's any free food involved.'

'Yeah, I'm sure that's true,' I smiled. 'Everyone likes free sweets after all.'

'It's not just free food, I think,' Becca added. 'It's something that catches their imagination. I bet you don't remember asking Ali in my class to try and memorise that series of pictures?'

'Which one?' I asked. 'The one of the different things people value? The iPod and PlayStation and money and all that?'

'Yeah, that's the one. Well, we were talking in class last week about important things, and I mentioned that assembly, and Ali was so proud of the fact that he'd managed to remember all ten. And that was right at the start of term, must be a good three months ago. But he still remembered that detail. Not sure if he also remembered the point about it's not just having stuff that makes you happy, but you never know, he might well do.'

'That's the thing about assemblies,' I said, 'You have to drip feed the stuff to them, and keep on repeating things over time, and hope it eventually goes in. Just like teaching anything I guess. I do hope we don't get any more stress about prayers though next term.'

'What do you mean?' Phil asked.

'Well, you know how some of the lads like Kamal and Amjad, just won't close their eyes for the reflection and prayer time. I've decided that I'll ask twice and then just leave them to it. If they're going to refuse to take part, then I don't want to make it worse for the rest of the school but having a battle of wills with those two while everyone else is waiting.'

'Welcome to my world.' Phil laughed. 'I realised that fairly early on with them. There are lots of things that there's just no point in getting stressed over, and like you say, them closing their eyes in assembly is probably one of them. I imagine with those two, though I've not asked them, that they probably think it's *haram* to shut their eyes in case they prayed a Christian prayer by mistake. They're always really concerned about things being *haram*. Doesn't stop them being nasty to each other and fighting occasionally, mind you. That was why I was pleased that they got to hear something of a different point of view yesterday, even if it didn't all sink in. It's that drip, drip thing we were talking about. They just need to hear there's a different point of view.'

'Mind you,' Becca added, 'there are all sorts of reasons they may not want to close their eyes. Some kids just get really nervous having to close their eyes in public. I guess they think everyone might laugh at them or maybe the people sitting near them will poke them, or I dunno, all sorts of things.'

'Yeah, that's true. I hadn't thought of that. At least this drip, drip thing does work with some of them, or else we'd all give up wouldn't we?'

'You're right. I think Nuh is one of the best examples of that,' Phil suggested.

'How so?' Becca asked. 'He's always been respectful of others, hasn't he?'

'Not at all,' Phil explained. 'You've only seen him these past two years, since you joined the staff. I remember when he first came to school. I was teaching year one then, and he was in my class. He was a right pain. He could not cope with being in a Christian school at all. Every time I taught RE, he would be disruptive. Every time I mentioned the name "Jesus" he would sit there with his hands over his ears, saying, "that's *haram*, that's *haram*."'

'What?' I asked. 'How can it be *haram* to mention Jesus? His name is in the Quran. That makes no sense.'

'What's sense got to do with it?' Phil asked. 'Sense isn't the point. Feeling comfortable, feeling safe, feeling listened to, respected, acknowledged. They're the point. And we did that with Nuh. Took ages. Believe me, there were plenty of times when he had to be sent out of the class, when he had to go to Chris' office, all that sort of stuff. But slowly he's changed. Slowly he's learnt how to cope with difference, respect it even. Actually,' Phil smiled as he remembered, 'he's really changed. The other day, when we were doing

103

RE, and we were reading the New Testament, he was so interested I had to tell him off for reading and not listening to me. Talk about a change.'

'Seriously?' Becca asked. 'That's a huge change.'

'Isn't it?' I agreed. 'I think I've seen him reading a Bible at break time as well, probably a few months ago. I remember going and asking him why he was doing it. And he said that he liked learning about other religions. Mind you, the next week he was reading a book on Greek legends, so I wouldn't assume anything about his interest in the Bible.'

'No, but why should we?' said Phil. 'My point is that he's changed hugely from a kid who would not even cope with the name "Jesus" to one who has enough respect for Christians to actually want to read their holy book. That's massive. Absolutely massive. It's changes like that which make the job worth it.'

At that moment, the bell rang for the end of break. 'Well, it's a testament to how good the staff are here,' I agreed. 'Thanks, Phil. It is all about learning to recognise and accept a different point of view. Thanks for letting me speak to your class, Becca. Have a good break, guys, if I don't see you,' I said, as he and Becca left.

Then it struck me: a different point of view—what about a different Muslim point of view. Would that solve the problem Chris had mentioned last week? 'Let's not do prayers in school,' I thought. 'Let's get them to understand other people's points of view.' I went to find Chris.

He was in his office, concentrating on typing something on his laptop. He looked up as I came in.

'I've had an idea about that request from Asha's dad,' I said. 'What we do is, we say no to prayers, and say it's exactly the same as with the *halal* kitchen thing: we'll provide *halal* food, but can't make the whole kitchen *halal*. In a similar way, we can't do prayers, but we can create the space needed for dialogue. Let's invite some parents, like Mr Hussain perhaps, to come in to an RE lesson. We can get their parents to model dialogue and respect. Maybe we could even invite someone from the mosque to come in.'

'That's brilliant,' said Chris, his eyes lighting up. 'I've been a bit worried about what to do, but that is a good solution. Let's stick with parents—I'm sure it'll be much more powerful if we get their parents in rather than some bloke from the mosque who they don't know who it is.'

'Yeah, you're right.' I agreed.

'I mean, imagine Kamal listening to his dad telling the whole class you should respect Christians. That's just the sort of powerful message they need to hear. Great idea, Tom.'

'Well, it was Phil's idea really. It was something he said in the staffroom just now that gave me the idea.'

'Well, it's a good one. I'll try and catch Mr Hussain now. It's nearly time for the end of school.' Chris said reaching for his jacket and buttoning it up. 'Have a good Christmas if I don't see you tomorrow.'

'Yeah, you too. Cheers, mate.'

Afterword

As I said in the foreword, this is a fictional account of a school, although its basis is in fact. My aim has been to provide food for reflection and discussion. I have listed below some of the central aspects of my thought, which hopefully have been brought out within the novel, but here are listed for clarity.

Christian schools: the term 'Christian school' means different things to different people. Christianity can influence school organisation in a number of ways: it can form the backbone of everything that takes place, or it can simply be a thin veneer that has little impact on the day-to-day life of the school. The Anglican church in England has two categories of church school: Voluntary Aided and Voluntary Controlled. The former are (in theory at least) more overtly Christian: the school governing body will have a significant number of Christians present and will be chaired by a Christian. The church is expected to provide ten per cent of the budget for maintenance of the fabric of the building. Voluntary Controlled schools also have Christian governors, but the chair may not be a Christian, and there is no expectation of financial contributions from the church. In my experience many Anglican schools tend to be Christian in aspiration and ethos, but do not consider themselves to be agents of mission or church growth. That is to say, Christian values are foundational to school life, influence pastoral care and so forth, but there is no expectation that children who do not self-identify as Christian might be persuaded to become Christian as a result of their schooling.

Hospitality: some are uneasy about this metaphor, but I find it a helpful one. It does have its limits: there are pragmatic concerns about class size, the dictates of the National Curriculum, and expected behavioural norms. Being hospitable does not mean you tolerate racism, sexism or any form of discrimination. Moreover the metaphor of hospitality is applied to religious, not racial or ethnic differences. Thus a Christian school acts as a host for Muslim parents and pupils, who are only passing through an institution that has existed before them and will continue to exist once they have moved on. There are significant differences between Christianity and Islam, and ignoring these can be dangerous. A good host is at pains to make her guests feel welcome, and does everything she can to make their stay a comfortable and rewarding one. Furthermore, a host will learn from her guests, and although there is an imbalance of power between guest and host, this should not become coercive or threatening.

The suggested reading list at the end of the book provides some stimulating further discussion of the topic, but there are also a number of Old Testament passages that deserve detailed consideration, including the actions of Abraham in

Genesis 18; Elisha's healing of Naaman in 2 Kings 5; and the books of Ruth and Jonah. The New Testament also makes much of hospitality of the stranger and outsider, especially in the ministry of Jesus. Examples include his discussion with the woman at the well in John 4 and his use of a Samaritan in his famous parable of enemy turned saviour in Luke 10, together with the challenging parable of the sheep and goats in Matthew 25. The controversies in the book of Acts and many of Paul's letters include, amongst many other topics, passionate debate about the inclusion of strangers and outsiders in the people of God. The struggle to be a hospitable church is nothing new.

Assemblies in a Christian school will necessarily be distinctively Christian, but this does not mean they have to be exclusive. Worship cannot be forced, and pupils (and staff) should be given the option of participating as much or as little as they want to. Within these parameters, there is a need for discipline and maintenance of order. I think it is best to distinguish the two. Thus the headteacher and staff maintain discipline when a visitor takes assemblies.

Food: although the issue of *halal* food does periodically make the headlines, it is not actually that complex. Simply ensuring the kitchens buy *halal* meat, that it is prepared and served separately and children have an easy means of indicating their preference (as for example with the different coloured trays I mentioned in the novel) means that everyone gets food they can eat. There can be issues over pork gelatine in jelly sweets or even some biscuits, but you just need to read the label. Halal jelly sweets are relatively easy to buy if you look for them.

Clothing: again this does not have to be a complex issue. The Muslim Council of Britain guidance document

Towards Greater Understanding: Meeting the Needs of Muslim Pupils, published in 2007, and available from their website (http://www.mcb.org.uk/) provides guidance on a mainstream Muslim view. Essentially if female pupils wish to wear a headscarf, then a school uniform one should be made available. The bigger challenges come regarding PE, although the desire for single gender classes (especially for swimming) is perhaps a greater practical problem for schools than the expectation that girls cover themselves.

Lessons in general: although I only made passing mention of the issues, for some Muslims (admittedly a small minority), the idea of music, art and drama lessons is problematic. If this issue is raised, then it must be handled sensitively and with respect. The core concern is that music does not receive explicit sanction in the Quran, and there is a clear prohibition on the representation of the human form, as to do so would be to assume the divine prerogative. Having said that, such issues are relatively rare, which is why I have not tackled the subject at length here.

RE lessons: provided RE lessons focus on imparting information and have no confessional element, then these should not be problematic. It is important for teachers to be sensitive to the beliefs of those in their class, and to allow children to express their own understanding of particular religious teachings. In particular some children may possibly be reluctant to draw pictures of prophets or other religious figures, although this has never actually been an issue at St. Aidans. As I mention in chapter seven, lived religion is normally far more important to individuals than doctrine, and just because a text book says Muslims believe something, that doesn't necessarily mean every Muslim child in the class does believe that. Prayer is a good example of this: the five daily prayers are one of the five pillars of Islam, and hence an obligation for all Muslims. But in reality, many people who live in the UK and self-identify as Muslim do not actually pray five times every day, any more than many people who live in the UK and self-identify as Christian go to church every week or pray every day.

People not problems: this is my guiding principle. All Muslim pupils are people made in the image of God, and are to be respected and treated as such. They may pose us problems, but these problems must not dominate our view of the people. Jesus loves and cares for everyone, and as his followers, our duty is to make that clear to everyone we meet in any way we can. We must welcome everyone as if they were Jesus himself.

Reflecting theologically: It is important that we pray and reflect on our practice in schools; everyone involved with schools who thinks of themselves as Christian has, at the very least an 'operant theology,' a way of making decisions and behaving in the day-to-day that is informed by personal convictions about God, the nature of humanity, and our place in the world. We should all strive to be the best witnesses for Jesus we can wherever we find ourselves.

Some possible reading

Bretherton, L. 2010. *Hospitality as Holiness: Christian Witness Amid Moral Diversity*. Farnham, Ashgate.

Cox, J. 2011. *More than Caring and Sharing: Making a church school distinctive*. Stowmarket, Kevin Mayhew.

Nouwen, H. J. M. 1998. *Reaching Out*. London, Fount.

Smith, D. I. and B. Carvill 2000. *The Gift of the Stranger: Faith, Hospitality, and Foreign Language Learning*. Grand Rapids, Eerdmans.

Smith, D. I. and J. K. A. Smith 2011. *Teaching and Chrisitan Practices: Reshaping Faith & Learning*. Grand Rapids, Eerdmans.

Sutherland, A. 2006. *I was a stranger: A Christian theology of hospitality*. Nashville, Abingdon Press

Thiessen, E. 2011. *The Ethics of Evangelism: A Philosophical Defence of Ethical Proselytizing and Persuasion*. Milton Keynes, Paternoster.

Troll, C. W. 2009. *Dialogue and Difference: Clarity in Christian-Muslim Relations.* Maryknoll, Orbis Books.

Volf, M. 1994. *Exclusion and Embrace: Theological Exploration of Identity, Otherness and Reconciliation.* Nashville, Abingdon.

Ward, F. and S. Coakley. 2012. *Fear and Friendship: Anglicans Engaging with Islam.* London, Continuum.

Yong, A. 2008. *Hospitality and the Other: Pentecost, Christian Practices, and the Neighbor.* New York, Orbis Books.

Anglican Reports

Three relevant reports produced by the Anglican church:

The Road Ahead: A Christian-Muslim dialogue (2002).

Presence and Engagement: the churches task in a multi-faith society (2005).

Generous Love: the Truth of the Gospel and the call to dialogue (2008)